ELISE

MARGERY SCOTT

CLOVER RIDGE PRESS

High Stakes Bride
Jasper's Runaway Bride
Mail-Order Melanie

MAIL-ORDER BRIDES OF SAPPHIRE SPRINGS

Miranda

Audra

Kathryn

Elise

Laura

Cassie

BRIDES OF COLDWATER CREEK

Josie

Sally

Anna

Beth

Willa

OTHER HISTORICAL ROMANCES

Emma's Wish

Wild Wyoming Wind

Rose: Bride of Colorado

MEDICAL ROMANCES

The Surgeon's Homecoming
Stranded with the Surgeon
The Firefighter and the Lady Doc

ROMANTIC SUSPENSE

A Time for Secrets
No One to Tell
The Stranger She Knows
A Question of Guilt

CHAPTER 1

The baby was crying. Again!

Jason Porter sat at the kitchen table, too physically exhausted, too emotionally drained to even lift his fork.

He'd had ten minutes of blissful silence and now Beth's screams filled the house for the fourth time that evening.

He set his fork down beside his plate and dragged himself to his feet. He had to go upstairs and do whatever needed to be done so that his daughter would go back to sleep.

No, he corrected himself, not his daughter. Another man's daughter, according to the note he'd found on the bureau after his wife, Irene, ran off with his ranch foreman, a man he'd trusted like a brother.

Today, he'd buried Irene, less than two weeks after she'd walked out on him and Beth. She and her lover had died in a town an hour's drive from Sapphire

Springs, and the only person who knew what had happened was Micah Ford, his pastor as well as being a good friend. He intended to keep it that way.

Dragging himself to his feet, he trudged up the stairs to the bedroom. Beth was standing up in her crib, her cheeks flushed, tears staining her face. As soon as she saw him, she stopped crying and reached for him.

Gently, he scooped her into his arms and held her close to his chest, her fine blonde hair tickling his chin.

"Let's see what's bothering you and then you have to go back to sleep," he said softly. "We both need some shuteye."

Whether Beth understood or not didn't matter. Jason would take care of this child—the child of his heart—until she no longer needed him.

A few minutes later, Jason kissed Beth's forehead and put her back in her crib. He turned down the lamp and almost immediately, the baby's eyes closed.

Jason moved toward the door, but something stopped him from leaving the room. Instead, he slid into the rocking chair beside the crib and watched his daughter's tiny chest rise and fall with each breath.

How he loved that child! From the moment Beth had opened her eyes, Jason's heart had overflowed with love. Finding out he wasn't Beth's real father hadn't changed that.

Somehow, though, he'd have to be both father and mother to her, because his heart only had room for his daughter. No woman would ever thaw the ice that had formed around it since Irene's betrayal.

His throat tightened, his chest constricting with pain and grief. And even anger that he'd never be able to confront Irene and find out why she'd deserted them both. So many questions he'd never have answers to.

"Zut!" Elise Dupont swore as the iron seared her skin.

Her mother's voice filtered through from the bedroom to the kitchen where she and her older sister were working. "English, Elise. We speak English in America."

"Oui, Maman," Elise replied, deliberately speaking in the dialect she'd learned in the small town outside of Paris where she was born. Even though she'd left France five years before, sometimes the French words burst out without her even thinking about it.

Her mother appeared in the doorway, her hands planted on her ample hips.

Elise grinned.

"If your papa were here…" Tears filled her mother's eyes and her voice shook.

Elise's smile faded. She didn't need to hear the rest of her mother's words. She knew them by heart, having heard them many times in the days following her father's death. If her father were still alive, they wouldn't be living in a New York slum, working twelve hours a day every day doing other people's laundry just to survive.

She gazed out through the grimy window, her father's voice echoing in her mind. "One day, ma choupette," he used to tell her when he first arranged for them to travel to America. "One day, we will live in a big house and you will have the pony you've been begging for."

He'd promised them all that when they got to America, they'd have a life of riches and luxury, but he'd died before they reached his promised land.

Instead of wealth, they'd found themselves living in squalor in three small rooms with very little food and even less money. Her mother had been determined that her daughters would be educated so that they'd always be able to support themselves, and had begun taking in laundry.

Still, there had barely been enough money, and Elise knew her mother had even gone without food for herself so that she could provide books and supplies to teach her daughters.

With her three daughters helping after their studies were done for the day, they'd managed to eke out an existence.

Juliette, the oldest of the three, was promised to a bricklayer and was planning to marry before the year was out. Her betrothed lived a few blocks away in a rundown tenement and seemed to spend most of his income at the local tavern. A few times, Elise had seen bruises on her sister's arms. Juliette had made excuses for them—she'd fallen down the stairs or hit her cheek on a cabinet door—but she'd avoided meeting Elise's gaze, a sign Elise recognized. Juliette had never been able to look someone in the eye when she was telling a lie.

Yvonne, her middle sister, was a little more than a year older than Elise and was now studying to become a midwife with an elderly woman who lived nearby. Lately, she often stayed at the woman's home in case they were called on during the night.

For Elise and Juliette, the days were long and filled with washing and ironing, leaving their mother to take care of picking up and delivering to their customers.

That was going to change one day, Elise told herself every night after she said her bedtime prayers. One day, she would have a big house. And space. She'd look out on green fields instead of buildings and look up into a starry sky, not smoke from the factories.

Yes, Papa, she whispered as she draped the shirt over the ironing board and picked up the iron. One day!

"It's been six months, Jason." Micah's voice, although gentle, was stern at the same time. "It's time to remarry, for your daughter's sake, if for no other reason."

The church was empty, the parishioners gone

after the Sunday service. Jason hadn't had the energy—or the heart—to attend church since Irene's death, so he'd driven into town that morning to talk to Micah, his good friend as well as the town pastor. He'd left Beth with Tillie, Micah's wife, and waited until everyone had gone home before he went inside.

He was tired. Bone-weary. Looking after Beth as well as trying to keep his ranch going was getting harder and harder every day.

Micah was right. He couldn't keep imposing on his friends to look after his daughter while he did his chores. He had a dozen ranch hands, but they needed supervision, and he couldn't very well take Beth with him when he went out to ride the fence lines or rescue cattle who got mired in mud after a storm.

Still, to marry again…

He looked up into Micah's kind eyes. "It's too soon. How can I marry again? You know what happened before." Micah was the only person in town who knew the truth about Irene's death. Jason had needed someone to confide in, and he'd trusted that whatever he shared with Micah would never leave his lips.

"Beth needs a mother," Micah said.

Jason knew that, but how could Micah even suggest he find himself another wife after what Irene had done to him? Before he had a chance to point that out, Micah went on. "I realize you've been hurt, but you need to put your own misery aside and think of your child. She needs a woman's touch, a woman's care."

"Micah—"

"And by the looks of it, you do, too."

Ashamed, Jason looked down at the shirt he'd put on that morning. A button was missing, and even though he'd tried to iron the shirt, it was still creased.

"If there's no one in town you're interested in marrying, I'm sure Miranda Weaver could find one for you. She seems to have a gift for finding the perfect wife for every man who's gone to her for help."

He'd heard about a few men in town bringing brides from back East, but he couldn't imagine doing such a thing.

"You should think about it," Micah went on. "Your little one needs a mother, and it wouldn't hurt you to have some companionship out there on your ranch, too, even if you're not ready for anything else."

"I will," he said, although he had no intention of even considering it.

Beth was fussy all the way back to the ranch, struggling to escape Jason's hold on her while he drove the wagon the two miles back from town.

A few days before, she'd learned how to get around on her own. She didn't crawl exactly, but bounced on her bottom while she propelled herself with her legs and feet. A smile tugged at his lips. It made him laugh, even though since she'd discovered she could move, every chore inside the house took ten times longer than it had before. If he didn't keep an eye on her every second, she'd go off bouncing through the house, finding every crumb that had fallen on the floor or trying to pull the tablecloth off the table.

Why hadn't someone invented a way to keep their babies corralled like they did horses? Even as the thought crossed his mind, he dismissed it. Putting a fence around a baby was a whole different thing. He chuckled at the mental image.

When he got home, he fed Beth her supper, changed her diaper, and put her to bed. With any luck, she'd sleep through the night.

Jason sank into the chair in the parlor, reveling in the silence. How much longer could he cope? Every day was becoming more and more of a struggle. Right now, Beth could only move small distances, but what would happen once she was able to walk? And run? How could he possibly keep an eye on her every minute of the day and still get his ranch chores done?

Micah's words drifted into his mind. Beth needed a mother, and he needed someone to take over the chores in the house. And, he admitted to himself, a little company would be nice in the evenings once the chores were done.

He'd tried to hire a housekeeper right after Irene died but hadn't been able to find one. Was it possible now? More and more people had come to settle in Sapphire Springs in the past few weeks now that winter was over. Surely there was a woman in town who'd be willing to help him.

As the room sank into darkness, he made a mental list of every woman he knew who might be suitable—and rejected them all for one reason or another.

But a mail-order bride? Was that really the only solution?

CHAPTER 2

The mouth-watering aroma of bacon frying met Jason's nose when he opened the door to The Blue Sapphire, the diner Miranda and John Weaver owned, the next morning.

He'd lain awake most of the night thinking about what Micah had said, and as the sun peeked above the horizon, he'd made his decision.

The bell above the diner door jangled. He stepped inside. What he wouldn't give to have the time to sit and have breakfast in the diner. But he didn't. Tillie had offered to look after Beth while he spoke to Miranda and he wouldn't take advantage of her kindness.

He needed to ask Miranda about finding him a bride, get back to Micah's house and collect Beth, and then get back to the ranch to start his day's work as soon as he could.

Miranda was pouring coffee for two cowboys sitting at a table near the back of the diner when he paused inside the entrance. She looked up and gave him a wave.

He waited by the door, and as soon as she was finished, she came toward him. "Good morning, Jason," she said. "It's not often we see you here in town this early. There's a free table over there," she added, pointing to an empty table in a corner near the kitchen.

"I don't really need a table," Jason said."I came to talk to you but it looks like you're far too busy—"

"Oh?" Her brows arched. "What do you want to talk to me about?"

"I heard… I mean, Reverend Ford suggested I come to see you about finding me a bride."

"I see," Miranda said.

He shook his head. "No…never mind…it's a bad idea," he sputtered. "I'm sorry. You're busy. I shouldn't waste your time."

Miranda's gaze shifted as she scanned the café. Then she turned back to face Jason. "I'm a little busy right now, but why don't I come out to your place after the breakfast rush is over and we can talk? I'll explain the process, and if you still think it's not a good idea, we'll forget about it. How does that sound?"

Jason thought for a few seconds. Beth needed a mother. He needed to put his own feelings aside and think about her first. It wouldn't hurt to at least find out what the process was before he completely dismissed the idea. Finally, he nodded. "Okay. I don't guarantee that you're not wasting your time coming all the way out to my place, but I'm willing to listen."

"It's a lovely day for a ride and your ranch isn't far," she replied. "I should be finished here in an hour or so."

"Hey, Miranda," a deep voice called out. "When's my steak and eggs coming?"

Miranda turned her head toward the cowboy. "Be right there."

"I won't keep you any longer," Jason said. "I'll see you then."

Just as she'd promised, Miranda knocked on his door a little more than an hour later. He answered, invited her in and offered her coffee, realizing as soon as he did that he shouldn't have. His coffee tasted like tar. He knew it but for some reason he'd never been able to figure out why he couldn't make a decent pot.

He almost laughed at the expression on her face as she tried to hide a grimace when she took her first sip. He thought about apologizing, but she spoke before he could.

"First," she said, "why do you want to marry again?"

"Beth needs a mother."

"Is that the only reason?"

Jason shook his head. "That's most of it. I do get

lonely sometimes, but I'm not ready for a real marriage. I'm not sure I ever will be." That was an understatement. He'd never be ready for it again. Irene's betrayal had almost destroyed him. He couldn't let himself care for another woman and give her the power to do the same thing.

"You're still grieving," Miranda said, "and there's no timetable for that. You'll know when you're ready, and I do think there are many women who are widows and would understand that."

Jason was tempted to correct her, to admit that grief wasn't what had turned his heart to ice. Instead, he nodded and kept quiet. If she'd heard the circumstances around Irene's death, she didn't mention them.

As she sipped politely on the coffee, Miranda told him about the other marriages she'd arranged and how she'd found the brides. He knew of some of the couples she mentioned, and they seemed happy enough.

"You can change your mind at any time before you send the train ticket," she told him once she'd explained how she would proceed if he decided to advertise for a bride.

That was reassuring.

"What do you think?" she asked once she was finished explaining. "Do you still think it's a bad idea?"

He ran his hand through his mop of shaggy blond

hair. "Well…since I'd have a choice, assuming more than one woman answered the letter…I suppose I could see if there's one out there who'd suit me."

"I think you're doing the right thing, both for Beth and for you." She grinned. "If nothing else, you need a woman who can make coffee."

Elise's gaze rested on the box of washing powder on the shelf in the small market near their apartment. She counted the coins in her hand. Her mother had told her she could buy something for herself if she had money left over after she bought the items on the list.

If her arithmetic was right, she'd have three pennies left over, not that she planned to spend them. Those pennies would buy something they needed later.

Voices from behind the row of shelves where she stood reached her ears. "Did you hear about Regina Draper? She went to Texas to marry a cowboy there."

"No!" another voice responded. "How … where did she meet him?"

"I heard she found an ad in a new section in the newspaper advertising for mail-order brides," the first woman said. "I'm going to buy it for my mother. She's alone now, and there aren't many men here who are willing to marry a woman her age."

"But to go all the way to Texas," a shrill voice put in. "And to marry a stranger…"

"I know of several women who've done that," the first woman said, "and if my mother can find a good husband, I'll do the same thing."

Elise was intrigued. She'd heard of women who became mail-order brides, but she couldn't imagine doing such a thing no matter how poor she was. Still, if her only choice was working in a brothel like some women had to do when they had no way to support themselves, she could understand why it would be worth taking a chance. Submitting to one man was obviously better than submitting to many.

She listened for a few more seconds before she moved away, thoughts of what she'd heard about the West filling her mind. Open spaces, clean air, maybe even a garden.

A new life. One that she could make her own.

It couldn't hurt to at least look at the newspaper the woman had mentioned. As she carried the boxes of washing soap to the counter where the shopkeeper was dealing with another customer, she caught sight of a pile of newspapers on the counter. Almost as if she had no control, she plucked one of them out of the pile and added it to the rest of her purchases.

She wouldn't show it to her mother, knowing she would call it wasteful since the busybodies in their apartment building gave them all the news they needed.

As she hurried home, she found her anticipation

of what she'd find inside the pages of the newspaper rising.

She wanted to get married and have a family, but even at her young age, she'd already given up dreams of a loving husband, children and a home of her own. She didn't have time to even meet a man, and those she already knew were struggling to make ends meet even more than she and her mother were. And she sure didn't want a man like her sister's soon-to-be husband.

Keeping the newspaper under her coat, she set the shopping basket on the table when she reached their apartment and hurried into the bedroom before taking off her coat.

She scanned the room. There weren't many places where she could hide the newspaper so that her mother wouldn't find it. Finally, she tucked it under the mattress on her side of the small bed she shared with Yvonne.

The day seemed to drag on forever but finally, she was alone. Juliette was out with her beau, Yvonne was with her midwifery teacher and her mother was asleep.

Taking the newspaper out from where she'd hidden it, she tiptoed out to the main room and slid into a chair at the table.

Her eyes widened as she scanned the ads.

Old and young. Doctors, merchants and business owners. Farmers, ranchers and miners. Even an undertaker, although she couldn't imagine being married to a man whose livelihood depended on death.

If she was seriously looking for a husband, she'd have so many choices, both of the type of man she married and where she wanted to live.

Then she saw it. The ad read: "Widowed Texas rancher, age 23, seeks gentle Christian bride aged 20-25 to help him care for his home and young daughter in return for financial security and companionship. If interested, reply to Mrs. Miranda Weaver, Sapphire Springs, Texas.

Something about the ad intrigued her. Was it because it was in Texas, where the woman she'd heard about in the market had gone? Or was it the thought of a little girl without a mother? Or was it something else?

He hadn't said anything about love or what he would expect from her other than cleaning, cooking and caring for his child, yet she felt as if this man and this child were her destiny.

Could she really leave her mother and her sisters and cause them more work than they already had? Could she really travel so far away from everything she'd ever known? Yet if she stayed, her life would never change. And if the marriage worked out, perhaps she could arrange to send for her mother and her sisters. Yes, she thought, in the long run, this might be the answer.

If the marriage was a mistake or the man wasn't the good Christian man he seemed to be, she could always leave. She had enough education and home-making skills that she could find work and save enough money to come home.

Before she had time to change her mind, she took out her writing supplies from the small desk in the parlor, sat down and began to write.

Jason sat at one of the tables in the Blue Sapphire early one morning three weeks later, watching Miranda scurrying around, waiting on customers until they left. Then she came toward him and sat down across from him. "There's only one letter so far," she told him as she took an envelope out of her apron pocket and put it on the table in front of him. "It's still very early, though, so there may be more to come."

He nodded, barely able to muster up enough energy to dig his fork into the steak and eggs he'd ordered. Beth had been up most of the night, and Jason had barely slept. Now he had a full day of ranch work ahead of him, and all he wanted to do was sleep. "That may be, but I don't have the patience to wait for the perfect woman," he said. "I'm desperate."

Miranda nodded. "I understand."

"And I can't keep imposing on other people," he went on. "Whoever this woman is, if she doesn't have a criminal record and she's young enough, she'll do. If I could have found a housekeeper or nanny, that would have been enough for me, but if I have to get married again to find someone to look after the house and Beth, then I'll get married again. It doesn't matter who she is."

"That's not really very fair," Miranda pointed out, "and I'm sure it matters to her that she's wanted as a wife, not a housekeeper. I'm sure she's hoping for a real marriage and that one day, you might fall in love. Every woman does."

"I'll take care of her, I'll be kind, and she'll never have to want for anything. That's all I can offer. I'm not capable of loving another woman."

"Then I suggest if you're going to write to her and propose marriage you should be honest."

Miranda was right. It wouldn't be fair, but at this point, he was desperate. Even with Roy and the other hands doing their best, the ranch was his responsibility. And he was failing, and if this situation went on much longer, he'd lose it all.

Still, he couldn't ask her to travel all the way to Texas under false pretenses. He nodded his agreement.

Maybe Miranda was wrong. Maybe this woman was looking for financial security and nothing else. Maybe she'd be quite happy with what he had to offer.

Miranda stood up. "Why don't I get you a cup of coffee and you can read the letter and then we'll talk?"

"That would be nice," Jason replied. "Thanks."

As Miranda moved away, Jason opened the envelope and took out a single sheet of paper. The letter was short, the handwriting small but obviously feminine.

Dear Mr. Porter,

I am writing to answer your advertisement for a bride. I am 19 years
old and live with my mother and two sisters in New York City but I was born in a small town near Paris, France and have lived in America since seven years.

I have light brown hair and brown eyes and have good health.

I help my mother taking in laundry and will like a new life in the country rather than in a town or city. I do love children and I will like to help you raise your daughter. I will like a marriage of trust and respect, and hopefully friendship.

I am a hard worker and will be happy to help you in any way that I can. If you think I might make a suitable wife for you, please write back. I can leave here on short notice and be in Texas within two weeks of receiving your letter.

Sincerely,
Elise Dupont

Jason smiled as he read the letter. He was right. She wasn't interested in love, only friendship. She was perfect for him.

"She's French," Jason told Miranda when she came back with the coffeepot and poured him a cup of coffee.

Miranda's brows lifted. "That's interesting. There are two other women in town that I know originally came from Europe, but I'm not sure exactly where they came from."

"She writes English, though, so she must speak English well enough."

"That's true."

Miranda wandered away, filled another customer's cup and took the coffeepot back to the kitchen. When she came back, she slid into a chair opposite him.

"Are you still planning to ask this woman to marry you?"

He nodded. She was a little younger than he'd planned, but not by much, and since it looked like she was used to hard work, she'd do just fine. "I am."

"So you need to write back and tell her more about you and Beth and your life here, and explain how you feel about marrying again. That way, if she decides to accept your proposal, there won't be any surprises."

"I'll do that."

"In the meantime, there will likely be other possible brides—"

"If she'll have me, I'm marrying this one. I don't need to see any other letters."

"Okay then," Miranda said. "If she answers that letter, then you send her a train ticket to Austin. You can either arrange for her to get on the stage to Sapphire Springs or you can pick her up in Austin and bring her to town yourself."

"That would mean more time away from the ranch..."

"That's true," Miranda agreed, "but I would still advise you to meet her in Austin. She'll be tired after the train journey, and having some time alone together will give you both a chance to get to know each other a little better."

He nodded. "That's true. I can leave the hands for the afternoon and I'm sure Tillie will take care of Beth while I go to Austin to get her."

"If you can, also send her a little money to help her with any travel expenses she might have."

"What if she takes the money and doesn't come?"

Miranda smiled softly. "It's possible, I admit, but that's a chance you'll have to take. I've never had that happen so far."

"Have your other couples married as soon as the bride got here?"

Miranda nodded. "That's not necessary, though. In your case, I think you should take your time since you haven't even considered more than one woman."

Even though he was anxious to get married so he could get back to work, it likely was a good idea to get to know her a little before he married her. After all, it wasn't just him that would be affected by this woman. He had to think about the woman who was going to be a mother to Beth. What if the woman wasn't at all what she seemed like? What if she didn't like Beth? What if he didn't like her even enough to spend more than the two hours they'd be together between Austin and Sapphire Springs?

He nodded. "Micah and Tillie did offer to let my bride stay at their home for a few days so that she could meet Beth and we could both be sure about the marriage before we said our vows."

"I think you should accept."

"I think you're right, and if it doesn't work out, I can get her a ticket to go back to where she came from."

"Elise? Come! Supper is growing cold."

Elise's mother's voice pierced the air in the small apartment where Elise was perched on the edge of her bed, an envelope in her hands.

Another letter addressed to her from Jason Porter in Texas. This was the second letter she'd received from him, and she'd yet to tell her mother about her decision to become a mail-order bride.

In Jason's last letter, he'd pointed out that he was still grieving after losing his wife and he hoped she understood.

She did understand grief, but from what both Juliette and Yvonne had told her, men still had needs no matter how upset or tired or angry they were. So even if he was grieving, she assumed he'd still have those needs and she might have the children she'd always dreamed of.

Yvonne had also told her that what happened between a husband and wife that resulted in babies could be quite painful for a woman. Still, how unpleasant could it be when women kept having babies?

She'd written back immediately, telling him she understood completely.

Slipping her finger under the envelope flap, she ripped it open, her eyes widening when she saw the contents—a railway ticket to Austin, Texas and several bills. Unfolding the single sheet of paper, she read his letter asking her to come to Texas to marry him.

"Elise!"

Her fingers shook as she slid the letter back into the envelope and tucked it into her apron pocket. Excitement, fear, anticipation—so many emotions coursed through her that when she opened the door and stepped into the main room, her mother frowned and gave her a concerned look.

"Are you all right?" she asked.

Elise nodded. How was she ever going to tell her mother that she was leaving, going to be a mail-order bride to a rancher so many miles away?

To be sure he reached the station before the train arrived, Jason had left Sapphire Springs at dawn after he'd dropped Beth at Micah's house. He'd reached Austin with more than an hour to spare, and it felt as if he'd been pacing the entire time.

Perspiration rolled down his back between his shoulder blades, as much due to his nervousness as to the heat of the day. He was nervous. He admitted that. He'd barely slept the night before, wondering if he was doing the right thing. Yet he couldn't see he'd had any choice. Even though he'd tried to clean the house up before she arrived, it was still a mess. The fences needed mending, and countless other chores around the ranch were being put off or ignored because he wasn't keeping on top of things.

He'd bought more land the year before and he'd been planning to hire more help, but after what had happened, he hadn't been able to muster the energy to do much of anything past feed and take care of Beth. Now it was time to get the ranch back on its feet. He only hoped Elise was the kind of woman who would be able to step in and take over the house and Beth's care so he could concentrate on the ranch.

"Elise," he whispered aloud. A pretty name. He couldn't help wondering if his new bride's appearance matched the name. Not that her looks mattered. He needed a housekeeper, nothing more. And if she was pretty, that would make it even harder to forget that she was a woman and he was a man. And if she was pretty, maybe she'd be like Irene and would leave him eventually, too when she found somebody better. Trust was something he'd lost and he doubted he'd ever find again.

CHAPTER 4

*E*lise sniffled back a sob and dabbed at her eyes with a white lace handkerchief her mother had given her. Oh, how she missed her mother and her sisters already.

Her mother had burst into tears when Elise told her about her plan, but she understood. Her sisters, on the other hand, were happy for her although she knew they'd miss her.

She'd spent much of the first few days on the train crying, but as the days wore on, her crying jags became fewer and she began to look forward to reaching Texas.

Until today.

She stared out the window as the miles and miles of open land passed by, the rhythmic chugging of the train's wheels taking her closer and closer to the man she had promised to marry.

Her stomach roiled. Her heart raced and her skin

felt as if a thousand ants were crawling on it. What had she done? It had seemed so exciting when she'd first decided to accept Jason's proposal but now… Now that the time had almost come to meet him, she was terrified.

She'd wanted to escape New York, wanted to build a new life away from constant laundry, but what if she'd made a huge mistake? What if he was cruel? What if he beat her? What if the leap of faith she'd taken was a leap into the depths of Hell?

Her thoughts—and her fear—filled her and she took a few deep breaths to calm herself before she embarrassed herself by losing her breakfast.

"This is your stop, ma'am," the conductor said as he came toward her and stopped beside her seat. "You can collect your bags at the rear of the train."

"Thank you," she croaked. Her throat was as dry as the dust clouds the breeze whipped up.

As the train passed a wagon standing near the station, a tall, balding man with a scraggly beard and a belly that strained the buttons on his shirt climbed down from the seat. He met her eyes through the window and grinned.

Mon Dieu! Could this be Jason? He hadn't mentioned his appearance in his advertisement but she'd assumed he would be in good physical shape considering his work. He'd certainly never mentioned being balding and overweight.

She was being shallow. She realized that. Hadn't she been taught that looks weren't important, that character and kindness were the qualities she should look for in a man? It was quite possible that he would give her a good life and perhaps she might even fall in love with him eventually.

As the train slowed to a stop, she got to her feet, picked up her valise and made her way to the stairs.

Someone had placed a wooden step in front of the opening, and she stepped onto the platform.

People hurried about, reminding her of the streets in New York. The man she'd seen appeared a few yards away, and for a moment, she was tempted to climb back on the train and go back to New York.

He smiled at her as he reached her, then continued on his way. She turned to see him embrace an older woman. She knew it was wrong to be so relieved, but she couldn't help releasing the breath she hadn't even realized she was holding in a loud whoosh.

Soon, the platform emptied, and as she stood near the rear of the train, her trunk beside her, she began to wonder if her groom-to-be had changed his mind.

"Miss Dupont?" The voice coming from behind her was low and deep, with an accent she'd never heard before. A small shiver swept through her at the sound.

She spun around and looked up into a face that was both rugged and refined at the same time. Blue eyes almost as dark as a night sky looked down on her with curiosity. "Are you Elise Dupont?"

"Oui…yes," she answered.

"Jason Porter," he said, taking off the hat that had shaded his face. His hair was the color of honey and brushed his shirt collar. A few strands covered his forehead, contrasting against his sun-bronzed skin.

She held out her hand, the thought popping into her mind at that same moment that perhaps it wasn't appropriate in Texas for a woman to be so forward.

"It's a pleasure to meet you," he said, burying her hand in his. "Welcome to Texas."

His heat swept through her and she suddenly felt weak. She'd never experienced such a sensation, and she couldn't help wondering if this was what Juliette had meant when she'd told her and Yvonne how she'd felt when she'd first met her betrothed. "Thank you," Elise replied.

He offered her a smile that reached his eyes. "I guess we should be on a first name basis if we're going to be husband and wife."

She found herself returning his smile and relaxing slightly. "I suppose we should."

He reached down and lifted her trunk onto his shoulder as if it were no heavier than a bag of dried leaves. "The wagon's over there," he said, gesturing with his head to a wagon and two black horses tied to a hitching post alongside several others. He began to move toward it. "How was your trip?"

"Very long," she replied with a small chuckle, "and I admit I'm glad to be off the train. It was such an interesting journey, though. This country... the rivers and the mountains and ..." She stopped herself, hoping he didn't think she did nothing but prattle on.

"It is pretty impressive, isn't it?"

"It is. I'm so glad I got the chance to see it. I haven't seen anything of America other than New York City."

A few seconds later, they reached the wagon and he deposited the trunk in the back. She watched as he set a foot on the hub of the wheel and hoisted himself into the seat.

Elise did her best to copy him, but somehow lost her balance. A split second later, she was sprawled in a tangle of arms and legs on top of him on the wagon seat. "Ohhh …"

His arms wrapped around her, pressing her body against his. "Careful," he said, "you're liable to fall out and hurt yourself."

Elise had never been so mortified in her life. What must he think of her that she couldn't even get into a wagon without creating a scene?

"Are you all right?" he asked, releasing his grip and helping her to steady herself on the seat.

She nodded, looking up and meeting his dark gaze. "I'm so sorry…"

"It's my fault," he objected. "I didn't even think you'd have trouble."

"I don't remember the last time I rode in a wagon. We didn't have room to keep a horse or wagon, not that we needed one anyway. Everything was close by, so we walked everywhere."

He smiled and an unfamiliar sensation almost like a fluttering filled her. Strange, she thought. *I hope I'm not becoming ill after being in the train for so long.*

"Looks like you'll need some lessons," he commented.

"I'm afraid I might need lessons about a lot of things," she replied. "I'm sure there's much to learn about living on a ranch rather than in the middle of a city."

"I suppose there is."

"I will be pleased to live in the country," she said a short time later as she breathed in an unpleasant odor she couldn't identify. "You wrote about your daughter. I look forward to meeting her and being her *maman*, but please tell me more about you and the rest of your family."

Jason slid a glance at Elise beside him on the wagon seat. She was looking at him, her eyes wide, a half-smile on her lips. A few strands of her light brown hair had come loose in the breeze and fell in loose curls to her shoulders.

She really was much prettier than he'd expected. Not a stunning beauty like Irene was, but there was a softness, a sweetness in her face that gave him a good feeling. And her voice … already he loved listening to her speak. A faint accent tinged her speech, but it gave the words a lilt that made him want to smile.

He'd already noticed that sometimes she spoke like they did in the books he'd read, and the odd time she used the wrong word, but it didn't bother him at all. In fact, he found it … captivating. "Well," he began, "there's not much to tell."

She chuckled, a musical sound he'd never heard before. "I am sure that's not true, but if you think so, then I shall ask questions and you answer, okay?"

"Fire away."

"You were married, is that not so?"

He nodded, but he wasn't about to tell her the whole story of his disastrous marriage. Not right now. Maybe not ever.

"I am sorry your wife died," she said.

He could hear the sympathy in her voice. "My papa also died. I understand your grief."

He'd gotten past the grief. At least he thought he had. It was the anger and bitterness he still hadn't dealt with, and likely never would.

"Thank you."

"But she left you a baby girl," she went on. "It must be difficult to care for her and do your work. This is why you need me."

He shifted to look at her. A wide smile curved her mouth. He did need her, more than he wanted to. "It is," he said. "Especially now that she's getting around on her own."

"She walks?"

He nodded. "She just had her first birthday last week."

"You have no family to help you?"

He shook his head. "My folks are gone. My brother, Travis, lives in Colorado but that's the only family I have."

"Then do not worry. Now I will care for her while you care for your farm and your animals. And of course I will care for your house as well and cook your meals."

"It's a ranch," he corrected.

Her brows lifted. "There's a difference?"

He nodded. "A farm in Texas grows crops. A ranch has cattle or horses."

She grinned. "I have learned something new already."

"About the house…" he began. He hated having to bring it up, but it was better she know what she was stepping into rather than being shocked when she saw it.

Her brows arched slightly. "Yes?"

"It's a mess right now. I couldn't manage to look after Beth and the ranch and keep up the house. I'm sorry you're going to walk into a lot of work."

She laughed again. "I am very used to hard work and I will be happy to take care of your house and your daughter."

He shifted to look at her. Was he really that lucky, or were her words just words? Was she going to be singing a different tune once she was living away from other people and her life was nothing but work and looking after a baby?

He hoped not, and he wanted to assure her he wasn't going to treat her like the hired help. "Once we're married, it'll be *our* house and *our* daughter." He'd thought long and hard about telling Elise about Beth before they got married, but how could he without telling her about what Irene had done? And he wasn't about to tell her that he'd been such a terrible husband that she'd run off with another man.

"When will we marry? When we reach Sapphire Springs?"

He shook his head. "I thought it might be a good idea for you to meet Beth and for us to get to know each other a little before the wedding, so I arranged for you to stay with Micah Ford and his wife, Tillie, for a few days. He's the town pastor and they're good people."

"You mean in case you decide I'm not suitable."

"No…that's not—"

"I believe that is exactly what you mean. If I should have a child, I will want to make sure the person who is going to care for my child is the right person as well. But," she went on, "I also will like to be sure you and your daughter are the right people for me."

She smiled at him then, and he couldn't help but return that smile. He got the impression that this was a woman who was going to be brutally honest with him, whether he liked it or not. And he had to admit, he did.

CHAPTER 5

*E*lise gave Jason a smile as she stood to climb out of the wagon in front of a small house ncar the town church at the edge of town. She shifted and suddenly, Jason's hands were wrapped around her waist and she was being lifted into the air. Less than a breath later, her feet touched the ground and he practically shoved her away from him, looking at her as if she'd burned him with a fire-hot iron.

"We're here," he said, avoiding her gaze.

Elise nodded to show she'd heard him, but her throat suddenly tightened. She was almost as nervous meeting Micah and his wife—and the baby, Beth—as she'd been meeting Jason. What if the baby didn't like her? What if she couldn't look after her properly? Jason had made it very clear that he was marrying her because he needed a mother for his daughter. What would happen if he changed his mind about marrying her?

Before they reached the front porch, the door opened and a woman stood in the entrance. A welcoming smile creased her face. "Come in," she said, taking Elise's hand and drawing her into the house. "I'm Tillie Ford."

Jason took off his hat. "Afternoon, Tillie," he said. "This is Elise."

"I'm pleased to meet you, Mrs. Ford." Elise stepped into the small house, the aroma of freshly baked bread meeting her nose. Her mouth watered. She hadn't realized how hungry she really was.

"Oh," Tillie said. "Just call me Tillie."

Elise grinned. "Then I'm very pleased to meet you, Tillie."

"How's Beth," Jason interrupted.

"Oh, she's been an angel." Tillie took Elise's elbow and ushered her into a large dining room where four places were already set at the table. "You must be exhausted and starving," she said. "Let's get you something to eat to hold you over until supper and then you can rest for a little while."

Even though she was hungry, Elise was anxious to meet the child that would soon be hers. "I'd really like to meet Beth," she said softly.

Tillie shook her head. "She's down for a nap right now, but she'll be up soon. You'll have time to eat before she wakes and you can meet her then. Now sit down and tell me all about your trip. I remember when we made the trip to Texas, but when we did it, it was from Ohio in a wagon."

"I'm sure it must have been much harder than mine," Elise said.

"I was much younger then," Tillie put in. Then she chuckled. " I'm happy to be here and not in any hurry to make that trip again."

At that moment, a man Elise assumed was the pastor entered the room. Jason got up and made the introductions.

"Welcome to Texas, Elise," the pastor said.

"Thank you, Reverend," she replied.

"No title," he corrected. "Micah to my friends, and since you're going to be Jason's wife, you're already a good friend."

He sent a smile in his wife's direction. "We prayed you'd get here safely, and we're both thankful our prayers were answered." Turning toward Jason, he added, "You made good time."

"I wanted to get back to Beth," Jason said. "And I knew Elise would be glad to get the trip over with."

Elise smiled at him. "I am very glad," she said.

"Well now, Micah," Tillie said to her husband, "if you'll bless the food, we can feed this poor girl before she faints dead away."

Elise sat quietly while Jason, Tillie and Micah made plans to build a new barn for one of the neighboring farmers. A storm the week before had blown the roof off.

On the way to town, Jason had mentioned that he'd had to neglect his ranch so that he could care for Beth, yet he was going to take more time away from his own work to help a neighbor.

Only a good man would do that, she thought. In fact, she'd only known one man who was willing to give of himself without expecting anything in return. Her father.

"I'll bring it up on Sunday, and that gives me a good idea for the subject of my sermon," Micah said. "Love thy neighbor." He smiled at Elise. "And also love our new neighbors."

Elise smiled, touched by his kindness, and then took a sip of her second cup of tea. Suddenly, a whimper filtered into the room from behind a closed door.

Jason got up. "That's Beth," he said with a grin. "She's awake." He disappeared into the other room, appearing a few seconds later with the baby in his arms.

Beth's pale blonde hair was mussed, her cheeks rosy. She was still sleepy, rubbing her eyes with her tiny hands, but when she looked over and saw Tillie, she grinned, her smile showing only a few tiny teeth.

Then she saw Elise and her smile faded. A frown creased her forehead a moment or two before she buried her head into Jason's shirt.

Elise's heart filled with … longing. She hadn't been around many babies, but something about this baby tugged at her heart. She couldn't wait to snuggle

Beth against her chest, but she knew it would take time for the baby to warm up to her.

A few seconds later, Beth raised her head and gave Elise a curious glance.

"Hello, Beth," Elise said softly, taking a step toward her and holding out her arm, making sure she didn't touch the baby but staying within reach of the baby's hand.

Whether it was Elise's slight accent or something else, Elise didn't know, but a smile creased Beth's face and she grabbed at Elise's finger.

Elise laughed, and moments later, Beth giggled and squirmed against Jason's hold, reaching for Elise.

"I can't believe she's doing that," Jason said, releasing Beth into Elise's arms. "She's usually pretty shy until she gets to know people."

Elise met Jason's gaze, the expression in his eyes unreadable. What was he thinking? Was he pleased that Beth seemed to like her? Elise wasn't sure.

Beth's fine hair tickled Elise's chin when she held the baby against her chest. Moving away from Jason, she wandered around the room with Beth to see if she would get upset if she lost sight of her father. She didn't, since she seemed to be fascinated by the locket Elise was wearing. It warmed Elise's heart that the baby seemed to like her.

"I'd better be getting back to the ranch," he said a few minutes later after watching Elise and Beth playing for a few minutes with a ball on the floor. He disappeared for a few seconds into the other room and returned carrying a bag. Then he picked Beth up and turned toward the door. "Thanks again for everything," he said to Tillie. "I'll see you tomorrow."

"Any time," Tillie replied with a smile. "You know we love having her."

"And I appreciate it more than you know."

"Are you taking the baby?" Elise burst in.

Jason nodded. "I'll bring her with me tomorrow."

"She can't stay today?" Elise interrupted. "I can take care of her. I do not have much experience with babies her age, but I will like to try."

Tillie patted Elise's arm. "I'm sure you'd be fine, but you need some rest after your long journey. They'll be back tomorrow."

Elise nodded. "I am a bit tired."

"I'll see you in the morning then," Jason said, moving toward the door.

"I will be looking forward to it," Elise replied, her insides warming at the thought of spending the day with Jason and his daughter.

So what do you think, Beth?" Jason asked later that night while he was changing the baby's diaper before putting her to bed.

She blew a bubble, then giggled.

"That's what I thought," he said with a smile. "You like her, don't you?"

He liked her too. He didn't know her well yet, but

after spending the two hours with her between Austin and Sapphire Springs, he'd already sensed that she was a kind, caring young woman who'd gone through a lot in the past, too.

He'd been surprised that Beth had taken to Elise the way she had. She was usually shy around strangers, and it took a while before she warmed up to them. Yet she'd gone to Elise without any hesitation at all.

Jason's grandfather had always said that children and animals could tell a person's character. If that was true, then Elise would be a good mother for Beth.

"She seems nice and might be good company for me, but if she can look after you, that's all that really matters."

Beth grinned and grabbed at his shirt collar.

He laughed. "I don't know why I'm talking to you about this. It's not as though you can give me any answers or advice."

Beth tried to wriggle away from him but he quickly grabbed her before she tumbled off the bed. "We'll see what happens tomorrow. It seems you like her, so I'll bring her out here with us tomorrow and see if she'll stay once she gets a look at the house. If I think she's capable of looking after you, then we'll get married in a few days and I can start getting things back to working the way they should be around here."

He picked her up and as he tried to enfold her in his arms, she jerked backwards, gazed up at him and swatted his nose. "I hope you don't do that to Elise," he said with a smile. "She might not be happy about being attacked."

Beth giggled.

Giving her a gentle hug, he laid her down in her crib, leaned over and kissed her forehead. "Sleep tight," he said softly as he turned off the lamp and left the room.

As Jason had promised, he and Beth arrived at the Fords' house the next morning. Tillie had offered to fill a bath for Elise the night before, and she'd gratefully accepted. Relaxing in the warm lavender-scented water, the tension and worry she'd felt since she left New York washed away.

It had been wonderful to feel clean again, and when she'd slipped into the freshly laundered sheets on the bed in the room Tillie had given her, she'd fallen asleep almost immediately.

Jason was standing on the porch when she opened the door, looking even more handsome than he had the day before. His pale blue shirt emphasized his tanned skin and made his eyes look even bluer. It was a shame Beth hadn't inherited those eyes, she thought.

"Good morning," Jason said. He smiled, his eyes crinkling at the corners. Even so, she could see the fatigue in his eyes.

Beth was crying, her cheeks flushed. "She's mad at me," he commented. She was bouncing up and down, swatting him with her tiny hands and squirming so much that if he didn't hold her tightly enough, she'd jump right out of his arms. "I've been hanging onto her since we left the ranch and she's not happy that I won't let her go," he explained.

"Then you'd better bring her inside." Elise stepped aside, a faint scent of soap filling her nose as he passed her.

As soon as he got inside the house, he lowered Beth to the floor and released her. She scurried away as fast as her tiny legs could go and grabbed a ball she'd left on the floor the day before. The tears stopped and a smile brightened her face as she held it up for all to see.

Elise chuckled. "She's much happier now."

"She's always happy when she gets her own way," he said with a smile. Then he sobered. "I have a feeling she's going to be a handful when she gets older."

Elise thought about it for a moment. "My mother always said my sister was a handful when she was growing up, but she's a strong, independent woman now. That's what you want for Beth, isn't it?"

"It is," he agreed, then laughed. "I only hope she doesn't drive me to an early grave before she gets there."

Just then, Tillie came into the room, wiping her

hands on a towel. "Good morning, Jason," she said. "Do you have time for coffee?"

"Thanks, but I want to get going." He moved to where Beth was playing with a piece of yarn from Tillie's knitting bag. He reached down to pick her up, but she looked up and gave him such a glare that he changed his mind. Elise had to cover her mouth to stop herself from laughing.

"Doesn't look like Beth wants to spend any more time in the wagon," Tillie commented. "Why don't you two go and I'll keep Beth here."

"I couldn't ask you—"

"You didn't ask," Tillie pointed out. "I offered. You both need to get to know each other if you're planning to marry, and you can't do that with a baby, especially an energetic baby like Beth with you."

Elise stood quietly nearby. It was an imposition for Tillie to keep Beth, but she did agree with her that she'd like to get to know Jason without having to focus on the baby at the same time. Still, she didn't feel like it was her place to offer an opinion.

"Okay, and thank you," Jason said finally. "We shouldn't be too long. I just want to show Elise the ranch and see if she thinks she'd be happy there."

"Take your time," Tillie said over her shoulder as she crouched beside Beth and tickled her with another short piece of yarn.

A few minutes later, Elise and Jason were leaving Sapphire Springs behind. As they rounded a curve in the trail, he slid a glance at her. "You're really pretty," he said. "You know that, don't you?"

Elise's cheeks warmed. She wasn't used to compliments, and she couldn't help being pleased. She'd been awake long before dawn, her excitement making it impossible to sleep.

After a light breakfast of bread and honey, she'd gone back upstairs to get dressed.

She'd taken special care with her appearance that morning, putting on the only nice summer dress she owned—light green and dotted with small white and yellow flowers. Then she'd brushed her hair until it shone. She couldn't tame her curls and waves so she'd tied them at the base of her neck with a green ribbon. She'd perched herself on a chair at the window and watched until she saw the wagon coming down the street.

As she'd hurried down the stairs to greet Jason and Beth, she'd pinched her cheeks to give them some color before she opened the door.

"Thank you," she murmured. Why was she suddenly feeling so shy, she wondered. It wasn't as if they hadn't met before. And he hadn't rejected her, so there was no reason for her to be so nervous.

"The ranch is just around the bend," he went on. "I should warn you, though, that it's been neglected for the past few months. Looking after Beth and the ranch …"

Elise reached out and rested her hand on his forearm, his corded muscles tensing under her touch.

"You don't have to explain," she said softly. "I understand. Grief changes everything."

He gazed at her, and for a split second, he seemed to want to say more and then decided against it. Instead, he just nodded and turned his attention back to the trail.

He'd have to tell her the truth about Irene and Beth one day. But not now. Not yet, while they were still getting to know each other. It wouldn't change anything, so he didn't feel as if he was being dishonest. And even now, after so much time had passed, his stomach soured when he thought about how Irene had betrayed him. And as if that wasn't bad enough, when she ran out on him, she'd left Beth behind.

That he couldn't understand. How a mother could leave her child was beyond him. He'd known one woman in town who'd left her son behind with his father, but she'd had a good reason. She was sick and was afraid she'd pass it on to her husband and baby. When she died, they found a letter addressed to her husband.

Irene, on the other hand, had left Beth behind because she didn't want to be a mother.

"Ohhh...is that it?"

Elise's voice drew Jason's thoughts back to the present. He slid a glance at Elise. "What?"

She met his gaze, her eyes bright and a wide smile on her face. "Is that your place?"

He nodded.

"It's … beautiful."

Jason looked at the ranch. He was used to it, the fenced corrals, the new barn he'd built the year before, and the two-story house with the wraparound porch. The yard had been neglected, and he'd meant to paint the porch before Elise arrived, but he'd run out of time. Still, looking at it through her eyes gave him a new appreciation for what he'd accomplished. And pride.

"So much space," she said breathlessly. "How much of the land is yours?" she asked.

"To the tree line over there," he said, pointing to a row of pines in the distance, "and to the river past where the cattle are grazing."

"And the house is so big … and beautiful," she gushed. "I will love taking care of it."

"About the house …" he began, trying to find the right words to describe the condition of the house. "It's been hard to keep it up …"

"Do not worry," she said, "I will fix it."

He'd tried to clean it up a bit before she arrived, but he hadn't gotten far. She had no idea what she was getting into.

A few minutes later, he tugged on the reins and stopped the wagon in front of the house. "This is it," he said, noticing the paint starting to peel on the porch posts and the weeds overtaking the flower bed Irene had planted when they were first married.

Elise climbed out of the wagon before he had a chance to help her, and she grinned. "I learn quickly."

"So I see."

"Like I said, the house is a mess and I'm sorry about that, but—"

"Can the things that are broken be fixed?"

"Well … I suppose so."

"And can the house be cleaned?"

"Sure, but—"

"Then that is all that matters. As soon as we are married, I will have it scoured and polished *en un rien de temps.*"

"Excuse me?"

He'd have to try to memorize the English meanings when she used a French expression so he wouldn't spend his life asking her to repeat herself. It might be a good thing for Beth to be able to speak another language, though. He made a mental note to ask her about teaching Beth one day. He laughed to himself. Since Beth didn't speak yet at all, there was still plenty of time to worry about what language it would be.

"Oh…" She chuckled. "In a trice. In no time."

Whether it was in French or English, it was easy for her to say that before she saw the condition of the house, he thought. He wanted to point that out, but before he had time to say anything more, she'd turned her back on him and was marching up the porch stairs and into the house.

Elise stepped inside the house. Just inside. *"Mon Dieu!"* The words escaped her lips on a soft gasp.

He'd warned her, but she'd truly believed he was exaggerating. He wasn't. While there was no sign anywhere that a baby lived in this house, it was quite obvious that a man—a very untidy man—lived there.

She could imagine what the large room had once looked like—sunshine streaming through sparkling windows, stuffed chairs waiting for someone to relax in, polished oak tables, and a clean hand-woven rug on the floor. Instead, a layer of dust so thick she could write her name in it covered the piano in the corner of the room, papers and books were piled on the tables, and clumps of dirt covered both the floor and the rug. Papers were even piled on the hearth of the stone fireplace that took up part of one wall.

"I'm sorry…" Jason's voice startled her. She spun around to face him. He looked away, as if he was unable to meet her gaze.

"You did warn me," she said, turning away and moving through the room to the large kitchen, where a table and eight chairs were also covered with bits and pieces of what looked like tools and strips of leather. Only one small area was empty. She assumed that was where he ate his meals.

Soiled dishes littered the counter that stretched the length of the room and pots still holding leftover food sat on the stove.

She shook her head. "I was wrong," she muttered. "It will take a little longer." A lot longer, she'd almost said, then stopped herself. Then, pasting a smile on her face, she added, "Will you show me the upstairs?"

His expression held a note of surprise. Did he really think that a little bit—or a lot—of housework would scare her off after she'd traveled half way across the country?

"Sure." Cupping her elbow, he led her through the house and followed her up the stairs to the second floor. She waited for him at the top of the stairs, unsure where she should go.

There were four bedrooms, but thankfully, only one, his room, was messy.

Strangely enough, Beth's bedroom was the neatest room in the house, although if it weren't for the crib and a rocking chair in the corner, it wouldn't look like a baby's nursery at all.

Still, it was clean and for that, she was thankful.

As if he could read her thoughts, he picked up a knitted shawl from the back of the rocking chair and began to refold it. "Irene was sick for the last two months before Beth was born. After, she had no interest in looking after the house."

"My sister is learning to be a midwife, and she has told me that pregnancy is difficult for some women."

"It was. Do you want to see the rest of the ranch?"

She nodded. Clearly, speaking about his wife was difficult for him even now and he'd deliberately changed the subject. She'd have to remember not to mention her again unless he did.

CHAPTER 7

*E*lise stood at the bottom of the porch stairs, her gaze scanning the open fields surrounding the house. A few wispy clouds dotted the clear blue sky and a soft breeze ruffled her hair, but she didn't care.

In the distance, animals roamed freely, and as she looked on, two men on horseback rode toward them.

"What are those men doing with the cows?"

"That's Abe and Bobby. They work for me, and they're checking to make sure none of the cattle are having any problems, that's all. Come on, I'll show you the rest."

He cupped her elbow and together they crossed to a fenced-in pen a few hundred yards away holding horses of all sizes and colors. Jason approached the fence and leaned his elbows on the top rail while he rested one foot on the bottom one.

Elise hung back, both fascinated and afraid at the

same time. Although some people in New York owned horses, no one she knew personally was rich enough to own one.

Poltron!, she muttered, then corrected herself. Coward! She'd left everything she knew and traveled hundreds of miles alone and she was afraid of a horse? How could she have possibly raised a pony without it growing into a full-sized horse?

Straightening and taking in a calming breath, she moved a little closer to the fence.

Jason turned and watched her, a frown creasing his brows. "Scared?"

"No," she lied.

"I didn't think so," he said, his lips twitching. "They won't hurt you if you treat them right."

"Are you sure?"

He nodded and held out his hand. She took it, his grip warming her and somehow lessening her fear. His callused fingers were rough against her skin, the sensation sending waves of heat up her arm.

One of the horses, a russet-colored beast with a white star on its forehead, wandered to the fence. Instinctively, Elise backed away.

The horse poked its head over the top rail of the fence. Turning to Elise, Jason smiled. "This is Rosie. She's my mare. She's expecting."

Elise's eyes widened. "How exciting! When?"

He shrugged. "No way to know for sure, but by the looks of her, I'd say within the next month or two."

As if the horse knew Jason was talking about her, she nudged his shoulder. He laughed as he gently massaged her forehead and then ran his hand down her neck. "She's pretty bossy at times."

"She's beautiful," Elise said. "When I was a little girl, friends of my parents owned horses. They were huge, like yours are, and I was never allowed to go near them for fear I might get hurt."

"Accidents do happen, but most folks get hurt because they don't know how to handle their horse. So I'm guessing you never learned how to ride?"

"Not really. When I was ten years old, one of the horses had a foal. My parents' friends allowed me to spend time with him but I was never allowed to ride him because they said he wasn't old enough. I begged my papa to buy me a pony of my own, a golden pony like one I saw at their friends' house."

"Golden? Like a palomino?"

She shrugged. "I don't know what kind of horse it was, only that it shone in the sunlight and its mane was almost white."

Jason stepped away from the fence and closer to where she was standing and Rosie wandered off to join the other horses. "I'm guessing he didn't buy you one."

"No. He told me he couldn't find one the right color."

"That's a shame."

"I didn't realize until I was much older that he couldn't afford to buy one but he didn't want to say so. When my father decided that we should come to America for a better life, he promised me that one day, we'd have enough money to buy a pony."

"And did he?"

Elise shook her head. "He became ill and died before we reached America."

"I'm sorry …"

"A pony was no longer important."

Just then, a man's voice called out from behind her. "Hey, boss, I need to talk to you for a minute."

Elise turned to see a tall, muscular man striding toward them. Lines creased his tanned skin, and a few strands of gray hair peeked out from under a stained Stetson. "Begging your pardon, ma'am," he said when he stopped beside Jason.

Jason turned to Elise. "Elise, this is Roy Keele, my foreman," he said. "Roy, meet Elise."

Roy gave her a wide smile, then reached up and touched the brim of his hat with his finger. "Happy to meet you, ma'am," he said. "I hope you'll be real happy here."

"Thank you," Elise replied. "I'm sure I will."

"If you need anything, just give me a shout. You can count on me and the boys to do everything we can to help."

"Thank you."

"So, boss …" Roy and Jason moved away to continue their conversation, and a few minutes later, Jason returned. "Sorry, but I need to take you back to town. There's something I need to attend to and it can't wait."

"No need to apologize," she assured him. "I've taken you away from your work as it is."

"I'm glad you understand."

A few minutes later, they were back on the trail toward Sapphire Springs. "Would you like to me to take care of Beth while you're gone?"

He didn't answer immediately.

"I'm happy to do it," she went on, uncomfortable under his scrutinizing gaze. "I don't know much about babies, but Tillie will be there to lend a hand if I run into something I can't handle. It will be good experience for when we're married, too."

He eyed her for what seemed like hours but was likely no more than a few seconds. Then he nodded. "That's true. And if you're sure you don't mind, I'd appreciate it. I'm going to buy some cattle. I was planning to buy them last week but somebody beat me to it. The sale didn't go through, though, so they're available again. I don't want to lose them this time. That's what Roy came to talk to me about."

"Oh, I hope you're not too late."

"Roy just heard about it, so I hope not. It's not far, just in Calico Creek."

"That's a pretty name for a town," she said. "So many towns in Texas have pretty names."

He shrugged. "I suppose so. I won't be more than two or three hours if you're sure."

Shifting to face him squarely, she gave him a confident smile. "I'm sure."

~

Jason heard the baby's giggles as soon as Tillie opened the door to him a few hours later when he got back from Calico Creek. "Sounds like Beth is happy," he said as he stepped inside.

"She is," Tillie replied. "Elise is feeding her right now."

"And she didn't have any trouble while I was gone."

Tillie shook her head. "She's a natural mother, Jason. Truly. And she and the baby seem to have formed a bond already. Beth was always quite shy, but she's taken to Elise as if she was her real mother. And Elise … she adores that child already. It's really quite remarkable. And you know you can always count on me to help Elise if she needs it."

"Thank you for telling me this," he said quietly. "So you think I should marry her then?"

Tillie looked up at him and nodded. "I think she'll not only be a fine mother but a good wife as well. I think in time the two of you will be very happy together."

"I appreciate that." He took a few steps toward the kitchen, then turned back to Tillie, who was absently rearranging a vase of flowers on the dining room table. "Would you mind taking care of Beth for a few more minutes? I'd like to take Elise outside and propose to her properly."

Tillie grinned. "Not at all. Would you like me to tell Micah that there's going to be a wedding soon, or would you rather speak to him yourself?"

Jason felt his face flush a little as he nodded. "Yes, please ask him if he can marry us as soon as possible."

"What is it?" Tillie asked. "What's wrong?"

Elise looked up from where she was sitting at the kitchen table. Tears filled her eyes and rolled down her cheeks. This wasn't how she'd dreamed of her wedding—in a burnt dress, in a strange town without her mother and her sisters to share her joy. In fact, there wasn't even really any joy.

Jason seemed to be a good man, and a good father. But there had been no declarations of love between them, only a proposal that had sounded as if he was hiring a housekeeper and nanny. Nothing more.

"It is ruined," Elise said through shuddery breaths. "My dress is ruined."

"What? How?"

Elise held up the dress that was supposed to be her wedding dress, the scorch mark plainly visible on the skirt. "I … the iron got too hot …"

"Oh, no …"

"Perhaps this is a sign that our marriage is not meant to be."

"Nonsense," Tillie contradicted, dropping into the chair beside Elise and taking her hand. "We'll think of something."

Then, a few seconds later, Tillie bounded up. "I've got it. I'll be right back."

Less than five minutes later, Tillie came back into the kitchen, a long pale cream gown in her arms. "This was my wedding dress," she said, her voice soft and melancholic. "I'm sure it'll fit you. You might not believe it, but I was once tiny like you." She laughed.

"Oh …" Elise gingerly touched the silk fabric. "I couldn't …"

"I'd be honored if you would …"

Tears filled her eyes, but this time, they were tears of gratitude to this woman who was quickly becoming a good friend. "Thank you."

Elise took wearing the dress as a good omen, seeing how happy Micah and his wife seemed to be. She hoped she'd be as lucky.

An hour later, she slipped into the dress and gazed at herself in the long mirror in Tillie's bedroom.

"You look absolutely enchanting," Tillie said. She'd styled Elise's hair and had picked a bouquet of flowers from the garden and tied them with a ribbon for her to carry.

Elise had to admit she'd never felt more beautiful. Although she and Jason weren't marrying for love, she couldn't help hoping that he would think she was beautiful, too.

Jason, Roy, Tillie and Micah were waiting for her when she came down the stairs a few minutes later, the bouquet of daisies Tillie had made for her doing little to hide her trembling hands.

Her gaze was drawn to Jason. How was it possible that he was even more handsome? His dark suit made him look like a businessman instead of a rancher. His shirt gleamed white against his tanned skin and he'd put on a ribbon tie. He'd had a haircut since she'd seen him last, and he'd even polished his boots.

Their eyes met, and she gave him a shy smile. He was looking at her as if he'd never seen her before. He returned her smile and warmth spread through her right to the tips of her toes.

Slowly because her knees were quaking, she made her way to where Jason was standing. When she reached him, he took her hand. "Ready?" he asked, his voice sounding gravelly.

She nodded. No, this wasn't how she'd pictured her wedding day, but this was the beginning of her new life and she was determined to make it the best life she was capable of.

CHAPTER 8

The wedding was short and passed in a blur. Elise must have said the right words, because before she knew it, the pastor—she had trouble thinking of him as Micah when he was performing the ceremony—was pronouncing them man and wife and telling Jason to kiss his bride.

Elise's eyes lifted to meet Jason's. His face was an unreadable mask. Didn't he want to kiss her? Was he still grieving so much that he couldn't bear the thought of kissing another woman? As yet another question popped into her brain, he lowered his head and kissed her. It wasn't a long kiss, a mere brush of his lips against hers, but it was enough to sear her lips more thoroughly than the iron had seared her dress.

Stunned at her reaction, she couldn't speak but could only gaze at him, wondering if he'd felt the same sensation.

He didn't say anything, their eyes locked on each other. Surely he'd felt it, too.

"Congratulations." Tillie Ford's voice broke into the haze in her brain. "I'm sure you two will be very happy together. Now come and eat before you leave," Tillie suggested. "You can't go without having a wedding lunch or supper or whatever you want to call it."

When they were finished their meal of roast beef, salads, freshly baked rolls and apple pie, Elise hugged Tillie goodbye. "Thank you so much for everything," she said, a lump forming in her throat. Tillie and Micah had shown her so much kindness that she knew she could never repay it.

Leaving the town behind a short time later, Elise sat quietly with Beth on her lap in the wagon while Jason drove.

Her nerves were strung so tightly she had trouble drawing in a deep breath, although Jason didn't seem to notice. Tillie had given Beth a rattle to play with on the way to the ranch, and Elise was grateful.

The sun was low in the sky by the time they rounded the curve in the trail leading to the ranch, shades of orange and scarlet streaking across the sky.

"It's as if an artist had painted it," Elise commented.

He nodded, but still didn't speak. Was he nervous? Surely not, since this wasn't his first wedding night. Still, he seemed tense, gripping the reins as if he were trying to control a hundred horses instead of two.

"It was nice of Tillie to provide us a meal so that I didn't have to cook tonight," she said. Strange that conversation was suddenly so difficult, she thought. They hadn't had that problem before the wedding.

"She's a nice lady," he commented.

Elise couldn't keep up a practically one-sided conversation all the way. "Is something wrong?" she asked finally. "You're very quiet. Are you having regrets already?" Or was he thinking about his wedding to the woman he'd loved?

He slid a glance in her direction. "No, not at all. I just …"

"Feel awkward?" she asked, her lips tweaking in a small smile.

"Yeah, I've been trying to find a way to tell you … that is, to assure you …"

She frowned. "What is it? Please tell me."

"I did mention in my letter that I wouldn't expect … anything …"

For a moment, she didn't understand what he was talking about. Then realization dawned, and a flush of embarrassment rose in her cheeks. "Ohhh …"

On the way to Texas, she'd had hours and hours to think of everything this marriage would be. Of course, she'd thought about their wedding night. He'd mentioned companionship and even though he hadn't said the words, she'd assumed he would want to exercise his rights as her husband. Then she'd deliberately put it out of her mind.

Now, she wasn't sure if she should thank him for

assuring her she didn't have to submit to him or whether she should be insulted that he didn't find her attractive enough to want to bed her.

"What I mean is, since we … our marriage isn't a normal one, I don't want you to feel obligated to … you know …"

She reached out and rested her hand on his forearm. The feel of his corded muscles beneath her touch sent warmth surging through her and she pulled her hand away. "Thank you for being so considerate, but if you do change your mind, I'm prepared to do my duty."

He turned to face her, his gaze so intense her throat tightened. "Elise," he said, his voice deep and strong, "if and when we ever do make this marriage a real one, I can guarantee you won't think of it as a duty, but as pleasure."

Her skin tingled and her cheeks flamed anew. How was she supposed to respond to such a statement?

Suddenly, Beth wriggled on her lap and swung the rattle, connecting with Elise's nose. While it stung slightly, it gave her the perfect excuse to focus on the baby and away from Jason and his breath-stealing words.

Jason turned his attention to driving the wagon, doing his best to avoid the ruts in the trail as they neared the ranch.

He'd been worried about bringing up the physical side of marriage, but Elise seemed to be quite happy with his decision. He'd never forced a woman to be intimate yet, and he wasn't about to start his marriage by making Elise uncomfortable or afraid.

Still, the touch of her hand on his arm, the expression in her eyes and the way she nibbled on her bottom lip affected him in ways he thought he'd never feel again.

He couldn't afford to let her slip behind his defenses. Even in the short time he'd known Elise, he'd learned one thing—it would be very easy to let himself care about her more than was smart.

Even their kiss after the wedding had made him start thinking about what their marriage could be, and how easy it would be to let it happen.

He wouldn't let that happen, though. He didn't need love. Didn't want love. He needed her, needed a woman to look after Beth and to take care of his home. He didn't need anything else. Sure, companionship would be nice, and if the past few days were any indication, they might even become good friends in time.

But that wasn't important right now. He was sending her into a mess to clean up, and he'd make a point of showing her how much he appreciated her.

"Tell you what," he said as he drew the wagon to a stop in front of the house. "Why don't you sleep in tomorrow morning? You've had a long trip and the past few days haven't been easy on you. I'll take care of Beth and make breakfast."

"That's really not necessary—"

"Maybe so, but I'd like to. You have a lot of work ahead of you and I don't want you to get worn out on your first day."

She chuckled, the soft melodic sound filling the air. Such a nice sound, he realized. He'd like to hear it often.

He drew the wagon to a stop in front of the house and quickly climbed down. Then he took Beth from Elise so she could join him. "I'll light some lamps," he said. "If you'd put Beth to bed, I'd appreciate it."

He turned to go into the house, then realized he'd forgotten to tell her one other important thing. He spun around. "There are two empty bedrooms. Pick whichever one you want. I'm going to take care of the horses and do my evening chores. It'll take a while, so I'll see you in the morning."

Roy was in the barn fixing a harness when Jason led the two horses in. "I'll take care of those for you," he said.

Jason shook his head. "It's all right. I'll do it." He needed some time away from Elise and taking care of the horses was the perfect excuse. She was too pretty, too sweet, too … everything.

He'd been shocked at his own reaction when he'd seen her coming down the stairs at the Fords' house for the wedding. Something had happened to him inside, a warmth and a sense of comfort that had unnerved him.

It wasn't lust. He knew what lust felt like. This was something different, something he didn't understand. And didn't like.

"Shouldn't you be with your bride on your wedding night?"

"She's still recovering from her trip." It was a lie, but if Roy recognized it as one, he had the good sense not to comment on it.

"She's a pretty girl." Roy hung the harness on a nail on the wall and took down another one to work on. "Friendly, too. All the boys think you did good."

Jason bristled. The last thing he needed or wanted was a woman who was friendly with his ranch hands. He hadn't paid much attention when Irene had spent time in the barn or talking to the hands. He should have, and he should have put a stop to it before it was too late. He wouldn't make that mistake again.

"Just remember she's my wife and not one of the soiled doves in the whorehouse in town."

Roy looked up, an expression of shock on his face. "What? You think any of the men would treat her like that?"

Jason had gone too far. "Sorry. It's been a long day."

"Go be with your bride and let me take care of the horses."

Jason nodded. "Thanks," he said, then turned and left the barn. An hour later, he was still sitting on the porch, trying to figure out how he was going to forbid Elise from having any kind of contact with his men.

CHAPTER 9

The aroma of bacon frying woke Elise the next morning. The room was bathed in golden light filtering through the curtains at the window. The sounds of activity outside the house told her she'd slept far beyond dawn.

She dressed quickly and hurried down the stairs. Jason was standing at the stove while Beth played on the floor beside him. As she entered, Beth lumbered to her feet and wobbled toward her with a wide smile.

Elise picked her up and snuggled her against her chest. She was amazed at how quickly she'd fallen in love with her. Beth's tiny fingers clutching her collar and her fine blonde curls tickling her cheek warmed Beth's heart.

"Good morning," Jason said, jabbing the bacon with a fork to move it from the skillet to a plate. "How did you sleep?"

"Fine, thank you," she lied. She'd lain awake a

good part of the night listening to the new sounds she knew she'd soon grow used to. "I didn't mean to sleep so late …"

"You needed it, I'm sure." He held up two eggs. "How do you want your eggs?"

"The same as yours will be fine," she replied.

His brows arched. "What if I like mine raw?" he asked, a smile on his lips and a teasing glint in his eyes.

"In that case, I prefer mine cooked," she answered with a chuckle.

"Over easy it is then."

While he cooked the eggs, Elise slid Beth into her highchair at the table.. Soon, the eggs and bacon were ready. Jason had also torn up a piece of bread and soaked it in egg yolk for Beth.

He set the plates on the table and took the coffee pot off the stove. "Coffee?" he asked.

"Yes, please," Elise answered, sliding into the chair beside Beth.

Beth snatched up a piece of the bread and popped it into her mouth, grinning. Egg yolk dripped off her fingers onto the highchair tray.

Jason laughed as he poured the coffee into a pottery mug. "She likes to eat and will eat almost anything, but this is one of her favorites," he told Elise.

"That's good to hear." She'd taken care of a friend's little girl once, and no matter what she did, the child refused to eat no matter what she offered. At least feeding Beth wouldn't be an issue.

She took a sip of the coffee and had to force herself to swallow it.

Jason gave her an apologetic smile. "I hear my coffee isn't very good."

"If you don't mind, I'll make the coffee from now on."

"That's fine with me," he said, dropping into the chair facing her.

"Do you think you'll be okay by yourself today?" he asked between bites. "Some of the boys rode down to get the cattle I bought the other day in Calico Creek. They should be here today sometime. I've got my eye on a new bull, too."

Elise really had no idea how much it cost to buy a cow, or a bull, or anything else in Texas, but she did know how much a small piece of beef cost in New York. She assumed a whole cow would cost a small fortune.

As if Jason could read her mind, he went on. "You look worried. What is it?"

"I know it's not my place to ask, but isn't it very expensive to buy cows?"

He reached across the table and squeezed her hand. "Elise, you have every right to ask. We're married now, and our finances are as much your business as they are mine. Okay?"

She nodded. "It's just that ... my family was so poor ..."

"I've been saving to buy the cattle and the bull for quite a while," he said. "We won't have much extra money until I sell off some of the beef next year but we have enough to get by."

"Perhaps I can find employment to help—"

"No." His voice was firm. "You have enough work here looking after the house and Beth. There's no need for you to work anywhere else. I promise you, we won't starve."

She nodded, then lowered her eyes and focused on her food, hoping he was right.

Jason hammered the nail into the fence post.

He was a happy man. In the short time that Elise and he had been married, she'd already scoured the house from top to bottom and had even started mending clothes that needed repair and knitting a sweater for Beth. Every night, a hot meal waited for him and usually, either a cake or a pie for dessert. And she'd taken over making the coffee, a blessing in itself.

But it was more than that. He enjoyed her company and her quiet grace. For the past few evenings, he'd been trying to teach her how to play backgammon. Finally, the night before, she'd won the game. Her eyes had sparkled and she'd bounded up from the table, clapping her hands in delight.

For a few seconds, it seemed as if she might throw her arms around him and hug him, but the moment passed and he wondered if he'd imagined it. He admitted to himself that he was a little disappointed.

Hearing Beth's laughter floating through the air behind him, he turned and glanced toward the house. Elise and Beth were walking toward a group of his men leaning on the corral fence. Elise was carrying something, but he was too far away to see what it was.

Memories flooded his brain and his insides twisted painfully. How many times had he seen Irene chatting with the men? He'd thought it was all so innocent. How wrong he'd been. He couldn't let the same thing happen again.

Straightening, he rubbed his soiled hands down his pants and marched across the field to where the men were standing. "You boys got nothing to do?"

His words had come out sharper than he'd intended. It wasn't their fault Elise had wandered over to speak to them.

And really, who could blame them for wanting to spend time with her? She was sweet and friendly, and that faint lilting accent in her voice was sure to mesmerize them the way it did him.

The men wandered away, leaving Roy behind with Jason and Elise.

"Something wrong, boss?" Roy asked. "You seem a bit out of sorts."

"No, not at all," Jason answered, forcing a lightness into his voice. "The latch on the corral gate is loose. Take a look at it, will you? I don't want to risk any of the horses getting out if it falls off."

"Sure thing," Roy replied.

Jason cupped Elise's elbow and led her away from the corral. Beth was playing with a ball in the grass nearby and Elise stopped to scoop her up into her arms.

Once they were out of earshot of the men, he paused and gave Elise a gentle smile, doing his best to keep his emotions out of his voice. "What brings you out here?"

Elise returned his smile. "I made shortbread, and I thought the men might like some. Why? Do I need a reason to be outside?"

"No," he blurted out quickly. "It's just that …" How could he say what he wanted to say without sounding as if he was accusing her of something?

"Just what?"

"They're men."

"I know that. What of it?"

"You're a woman …"

She laughed then, that full laugh that warmed his insides. "I know that too."

"A beautiful woman." As the words left his lips, he realized he meant it. He'd always thought she was pretty, but somehow, she'd changed. Or was it him who'd changed?

A flush rose on her face, making her even prettier than usual.

"I don't want you talking to them," he went on.

Her brow creased in a frown. "Why not?"

He wasn't about to risk history repeating itself and

Elise running off with another man once she got tired of living on the ranch. She was being far too friendly as it was. "They might get the wrong idea—"

She took a step back and gazed up at him. "You are being silly. They know I'm a married woman and I was only bringing them a treat. I'm sure they don't make dessert in the bunkhouse."

"Just the same—" he began, but it was too late. She'd already spun away from him and marched off toward the house.

Jason watched her go. Silly? She'd called him silly? No one, especially a woman, had ever called him silly, and he didn't like it.

The bigger question was, was she going to listen to him?

"I'll be in the house today doing some paperwork if you'd like to go into town by yourself." Jason chuckled. "Believe me, it's a lot easier to shop without having to deal with Beth at the same time."

Elise looked up from the dough she was kneading on the kitchen table. Jason was standing in the kitchen doorway, Beth in his arms. "Oh … yes … I will love to, but the bread—"

She'd been hoping to make a trip to the mercantile since their supplies were getting low, but she wondered if she should spend money when Jason had just bought the cows and the bull. "I do need flour and sugar, but I will not spend anything more than necessary."

Jason put Beth down and closed the gap between them. "You don't need to worry about money. Buy what you need. Okay?"

She nodded. "I am sorry," she said softly. "I … we struggled so much in New York, and it is difficult for me to let go of the worry, but I will try."

"Would it make you feel any better if you see the records?"

"What records?"

"The ranch is a business. I keep records of what I spend, what I earn. If it'll help ease your mind, I'll show them to you."

"That is not necessary. I will trust you to take care of us."

He smiled and her heart warmed. He really did have a nice smile, and it seemed he was smiling more and more every day. Was it possible he was starting to care for her as much as she was beginning to care for him?

CHAPTER 10

After lunch, Elise set off toward town. Jason had taught her how to drive the wagon and control the horses, but this was the first time she was alone.

A few dark clouds hung in the sky but she refused to worry about a possible storm before she got home. She loved Beth as much as if she were her own child, but she had to admit caring for a child, especially a child as curious and energetic as Beth, was time-consuming. It would be nice to have a few minutes to herself.

By the time she drew the wagon to a stop in front of the mercantile, the sky had darkened and as she stepped down onto the boardwalk, a gust of wind whipped down the street.

The bell above the door jingled as she hurried into the store. Coffee, spices, leather and even kerosene— scents mingled together in her nose.

The clerk was a beautiful young woman with pale blonde hair and eyes that were somewhere between gray and blue. She was weighing flour behind the counter, then pouring it into paper bags with writing on the outside and setting them aside.

Elise watched for a few seconds. She'd never known a store clerk to measure something out before it was sold. She supposed that was one of many things that were different here in the west.

Three ladies were discussing the merits of steaming vegetables over boiling them, while two men sat at a table near the pot-bellied stove in the back corner, a checkerboard between them. As she looked on, a man approached the woman at the counter.

While Elise waited for the man to finish his business, she wandered through the store, surprised at the number of goods available in the small space. She'd expected to have very few choices so far from a major city, yet everything from food to tools to kitchen gadgets and toys covered the shelves lining the walls.

She paused to admire the selection of fabrics piled on a shelf and plucked out a length of pale yellow flowered cotton. It would make such a pretty dress, she thought, but until Jason assured her they could afford it, she wouldn't spend money on anything other than necessities.

Noticing that the man had left the store, she put the fabric back on the shelf and crossed to the counter. "Good morning."

The clerk smiled at her. "Good morning," she

said. "I haven't seen you before. Are you new in town?"

"Yes, I am," Elise replied. "My name is Elise Dupont … I mean Porter." Elise giggled. "I recently married and I am not used to my new name yet."

The clerk's eyes widened. "You're Jason's new bride? Well … I must say you're much prettier than the last one." The woman's cheeks flushed. "Oh … I'm so sorry, I sometimes speak before I think."

"There is no need to apologize. I often do the same."

The two women shared a soft laugh.

"Well, then, welcome to Sapphire Springs," the woman said. "I'm Dorothea Jones. My family owns the store. What can I get for you this morning?"

Elise gave her the list she'd made earlier. Dorothea scanned it and nodded. "It may take a few minutes."

"Then I will take a walk and come back, if you do not mind."

"Not at all."

Elise left the store and strolled down the boardwalk toward the church at the edge of town. She paused to admire a hat in the milliner's shop window, passed the doctor's office and a gunsmith's shop, a diner and several other small businesses.

When she reached the church, she opened the door and went inside, hoping Micah would be there so she could say hello.

The building was empty, the stained glass window above the pulpit drawing her attention. She moved to the front and slipped into a pew, a sense of peace washing over her.

She was a lucky woman. She had a home, a good man who provided for her, and even though Beth wasn't a child of her body, she couldn't be more hers.

She was thankful for her blessings, but still, she wasn't content. She missed her mother and her sisters dreadfully, and lately, she'd realized she missed something she'd never had, and would never have—a husband's love. Jason's love. Her heart squeezed painfully.

"Stop it," she chided herself, speaking into the silence. Feeling sorry for herself was not going to help. She'd gone into this marriage with her eyes open, knowing he was still grieving. She'd accepted that, but lately … lately she was finding she wanted more.

She was falling in love with him. She wanted a real marriage, and possibly more children one day.

But that wasn't in her future, and no amount of wishing would make it so.

She rose from the pew, and as she left the church, she looked up. The sky had darkened to slate gray. If she didn't hurry, she wouldn't get back to the ranch before the rain started.

As the thought crossed her mind, the first raindrop landed on her nose. Within seconds, the wind swirled around her skirt and heavy rain pelted down, soaking her through.

She walked quickly down the boardwalk, and as she passed the saloon, a faint sound like someone sobbing broke through the wind whipping down the alley.

She paused, squinted into the dim light and saw movement. It wasn't an animal, but a girl on the ground, curled into a ball.

She couldn't go on and leave the girl there without making sure she wasn't hurt. She was soaked through now, so a little more rain wasn't going to make her any wetter.

Carefully picking her way around trash and mud to reach the girl, she crouched beside her. The girl's dark hair was drenched and fell around her shoulders. Her face was pale, and the blue satin dress she was wearing clung to her.

"Are you all right?" Elise asked.

The girl looked up, her dark brown eyes wide with fear, and scrambled further into the wall away from Elise.

"I'm not going to hurt you," Elise said softly. "Do you need help?"

The girl stared at her but didn't speak.

"Why are you out here like this?"

"Pas parle Anglais." Her voice was little more than a whisper when she answered.

Elise was stunned that there would be another French-speaking person in town. The difference was that this girl didn't speak English at all.

"My name is Elise," Elise said, easily slipping into her native language. "What's yours?"

The girl's face brightened. "You understand me?"

Elise nodded.

"I am Georgette Raynaud."

Elise repeated her question.

Haltingly at first, the girl began her story. "My mother brought me here to live with my uncle a few months ago."

"From where? Paris?"

She shook her head. "No, I come from Belgium. Our language is French."

"What happened?" Elise asked.

A gust of whipped through the alley, stirring up paper and bringing with it the stench of rotting cabbage.

"When we arrived, we found out he was gone. He didn't tell anyone where he was going. We had no money and no food. My mother began to work in the saloon, but she was killed three weeks ago. Mr. Long forced me to …" Georgette shook her head as if she were trying to erase the memories. "When I said no … no more … he told me I had to leave."

Anger churned in Elise's stomach. How could someone be so cruel?

"How long have you been living this way?" Elise asked.

"Several days now."

"When was the last time you had something to eat?"

Georgette shrugged. "A while, but I will eat again soon. I will go back. I have found it is no safer to be alone."

Elise was horrified. The girl didn't have to explain what she meant. It wasn't safe anywhere for a young woman to be alone outdoors after sunset.

Elise worried her bottom lip, something she found herself doing whenever she was worrying about something. She'd been trying hard to break the habit, but so far, she hadn't been able to.

It broke her heart to leave the girl in the alley, but she had no choice. She was tempted to take Georgette back to the ranch with her but she couldn't do that without talking to Jason first.

However, there was one thing she could do, at least for now. Digging into her reticule, she took out a few coins. Surely she could do without a few pennies. If she had to, she'd cut back on her purchases at the mercantile the next time she came to town. She, Jason and Beth wouldn't starve. Georgette could.

Taking the girl's hand, she pressed the coins into her palm. "Go and buy something to eat and then try to find somewhere warm and dry. I'll come back and help you as soon as I can. I just don't know how yet."

Giving Georgette's hand a hopeful squeeze, Elise left the alley. Her mind spun with ideas of how to help the unfortunate girl as she hurried through the rain to the mercantile and charged inside, her breath coming in short gasps as she closed the door behind her.

She'd planned to ask Dorothea if she knew the girl, but for some reason she couldn't even name, she'd changed her mind before she reached the mercantile.

Dorothea looked up, her eyes widening at Elise's appearance. "Oh my," she breathed.

"I got caught out there," Elise said, then groaned inwardly. As if she needed to explain why she was dripping wet. "I am sorry for the puddle I'm making."

Dorothea waved away her apology. "I'm used to wet floors. You should stay here until the rain stops."

"Oh, no, I can't do that. I have to get home. Besides, it's only water and I can't get any wetter."

Dorothea chuckled. "You can't, but your groceries can. Do you have somewhere to keep them dry?"

"I don't know," she replied. "There's a piece of canvas folded in the wagon bed but I'm not sure how big it is or if that will keep everything dry."

"That's probably why it's there, to keep things dry in the rain, so it like is big enough," Dorothea assured her. "I'll get your order."

After paying for her purchases, Elise hurried outside, tucked the basket and the other packages beneath the canvas in the wagon bed, climbed into the wagon and flicked the reins.

Thunder rolled in the distance, and a few seconds later, lightning flashed. It wasn't wise to be outside during a thunderstorm, and she sent up a small prayer that she'd be able to get home before it got any closer.

CHAPTER 11

Jason missed Elise. It shocked him, and he wasn't happy about it. Even though he'd been busy the whole afternoon, she hadn't been far from his thoughts.

His heartbeat quickened when he heard the rattle of the wagon outside. He bounded up, tossing his pencil on the table, and hurried out.

The rain had lessened to a soft drizzle, but Elise was soaked. Her clothes clung to her curves, and her wet hair, now a chestnut color because of the rain, hung almost to her waist. Raindrops even dripped off her nose and eyelashes. She shivered.

"Go upstairs and get out of those wet clothes while I heat water for you to have a hot bath," he said as he lifted the basket and the rest of her purchases out of the wagon bed.

"That's really not necessary—"

"You're going to catch pneumonia if you don't get

warm and dry soon," he interrupted, climbing the stairs and going back into the house, "and I don't want to risk you getting sick."

He needed her to be healthy to look after Beth and take care of the house, he told himself, but deep down, he knew that wasn't the only reason.

He was starting to like Elise—too much. The thought of her being ill bothered him more than he wanted to admit.

Elise followed him inside and closed the door behind her. "But I need to talk to you," she insisted.

"After your bath."

She let out a resigned sigh. "Fine."

Two hours later, he glanced up from the newspaper he was reading as Elise came back downstairs. She'd changed into a pale blue blouse and dark blue skirt and even though her hair was still wet, she'd tied it back with a ribbon, leaving her neck bare.

He had a sudden urge to kiss her, to taste that creamy skin on her neck. His throat dried up and heat surged through him. Heat he had no business feeling, he reminded himself.

"Thank you for the bath," she said as she came into the main room. "I do feel much better now."

"Good," he croaked out.

"I'll get supper started," she said as she passed him, the scent of lavender reaching his nose.

Throwing the newspaper down, he got to his feet. "I'm going out to the barn. I'll be back for supper."

Without giving her another look, he stormed out

the door, swearing under his breath that this marriage —a marriage in name only—was not working out the way he planned at all.

He hadn't planned to like her, to worry about her health other than how it affected her ability to look after Beth and the house, to miss her when they weren't together.

The question was, what was he going to do about it? She'd come to Texas for financial security. No other reason.

He thought back to their conversation when she'd first arrived about having a real marriage. She'd been more than agreeable when he'd told her he was willing to have a relationship with no marriage bed involved.

Now, he wished he'd never mentioned it.

But he had, and now, he regretted it. He wanted more, wanted her to feel the same way about him that he was starting to feel about her.

He wanted a real marriage, which brought him back to his original question—what was he going to do?

Elise was adding the last of the vegetables to the roasting pan when she heard the baby stirring. She hurried in and brought her into the main room. Beth busied herself playing with a rag doll Tillie had given her and Elise picked up her knitting while supper cooked.

She was thickening the gravy a while later when she heard the door open and Jason's boots on the wood floor as he crossed to the kitchen doorway.

"Smells good," he said as if nothing had happened.

"It's ready now."

While he settled Beth at the table, she carved the chicken she'd roasted and served the meal.

Jason seemed preoccupied during the meal, offering little conversation, so Elise focused on Beth while they ate.

"Now, what was it you wanted to talk to me about?" he asked once he'd finished his meal and was drinking his second cup of coffee.

She was pleased he'd remembered, but as she recounted the events of the afternoon, his expression changed and his eyes darkened.

"I'd like to help her," she said when she was finished. "Maybe I can bring her here until—"

"No."

Elise was surprised at the tone of his voice. She'd been sure he'd be willing to help. "Why not?"

He took a sip of coffee, then set the cup back on the saucer. He stared at it for a few seconds before he answered. "Look, Elise," he began. "I know you want to help this girl, and I'd like to help her, too, but I can't afford to support another person right now."

"Oh …" She hadn't thought about the extra cost of feeding Georgette.

"And she's a soiled dove," Jason added.

Elise bristled. She'd never thought Jason was a judgmental man.

"Only because she's had no choice."

"That may be true, but I'd bet every woman in the saloon is there because she had no choice. This girl, Georgette, is no different."

Elise hadn't really considered that, but she had to agree. She couldn't imagine any woman doing "that" if she had any other way to earn a living.

Still, something about this girl had touched Elise's heart, and she couldn't leave her to be used by the men who frequented the saloon.

"But she's so young, and she'll never be able to find work if she can't speak English …" she persisted.

"I'm sorry, Elise. I'd like to help her too, but we can't right now. And you can't save them all."

"I know." Elise let out a resigned sigh.

"There's something else you haven't thought about," he said. "You're new here and you haven't made friends yet. The women in town—"

It dawned on Elise what he was going to say, and she refused to listen to it. "If the women here shun me because I helped someone less fortunate than I am, I'm not interested in their friendship."

"I agree with you, but you need to think about that, and about Beth. Right now it doesn't matter because she's young, but once she's older, she'll want friends. What you do will affect Beth, too."

He was right. Many people had closed minds, but

how could she live with herself if she let others determine how she lived her life?

She couldn't turn her back on Georgette, but surely not everyone in town had closed minds. Still, she had to think about Beth. The whole situation bothered her so much it filled her thoughts for the rest of the night.

Elise quickly added a half dozen slices of bacon to the heated skillet a few mornings later. While they were cooking, she mixed up a bowl of pancake batter, ready to make when Jason came inside from his morning chores.

He was smiling when he came in. "I've been thinking," he said to Elise as she poured the pancake batter into the skillet.

Her stomach twitched as memories surfaced. Whenever her father had said those words, those "thoughts" had always ended with a decision he'd made that would change her life. His last thought had ultimately caused his death.

Her nerve endings tingled, and her chest tightened. "Oh?" she murmured past the sudden dryness in her throat.

"It's time we started going to church."

"Church?" she repeated.

"I—we used to go, but after Irene …"

Elise moved closer to him and rested her hand on

his shoulder. "I understand, and I'm glad you've reached the point you want to start going to Sunday services again."

In all the time Elise had been in Sapphire Springs, he'd rarely mentioned his wife. She hadn't wanted to pry, knowing that for some people, talking about the person they'd lost was too painful.

"That's not all," he went on.

"Oh?"

"If you're not too busy today, I want to take you into town."

That was unexpected, but a nice surprise. "Why?"

"You haven't met Miranda yet, and if it wasn't for her, you wouldn't be here."

Elise had been too busy until now to think about meeting any of the ladies in town, but if she was going to spend her life here, she wanted to have friends. Meeting the woman who'd placed the newspaper ad was a start.

She smiled. "I'd love to."

Elise's eyes widened. "You have three young children and you still manage to work?"

"That's right," Miranda replied.

Elise and Jason were sitting at a table in the kitchen of the Blue Sapphire visiting with Miranda and John Weaver. Beth was in a highchair beside the table eating—and playing with—a cookie.

"I couldn't run the diner without her," John put in from where he was standing at the stove stirring a pot of soup.

"Where are the children now?" Elise asked.

"John's aunt is looking after them today," Miranda said.

Elise took a sip of the tea Miranda had made. Her throat tightened. "Having family close by …" She let the words die on her lips.

Family. She'd likely never see her sisters and her mother again. Blinking back the tears that threatened to spill over, she forced herself to listen to what Miranda was saying.

"…and some of the ladies get together for a luncheon every few weeks. You'd be more than welcome to come if you'd like to meet some of them."

Jason gave her a supportive nod. "You should go. I'll take care of Beth."

"I'd like that," Elise said. "Thank you for the invitation."

Miranda took another cookie and broke it in half. "I'll send a message out to the ranch when the date is decided," she said and then popped half the cookie into her mouth.

Jason stood up. "It's getting late. We'd better be going. I have chores to do while there's still some daylight."

Miranda took Elise's hand in hers. "I'm so glad you came to visit. I'm sure we're going to be good friends."

"I think so too," Elise responded. "And thank you for the coffee and cookies. I'll see you again soon."

The bell above the door jangled. Miranda hurried out with Jason and Elise behind her. Dorothea was in the dining area. She smiled at Miranda. "I thought that was Jason's wagon outside." She held out an envelope. "This came for you. I hoped I could catch you before you left town to give it to you."

Elise took the envelope. Her heart swelled and a lump formed in her throat when she recognized the elegant handwriting. "It's from my mother."

Dorothea grinned. "Then I'm doubly glad I could get it to you."

So was Elise, and she couldn't wait to get back to the ranch to read all the news from back East.

Yet as she rode through town in the wagon with Jason and Beth, her mother's letter was the furthest thing from her mind. Instead, she found herself searching for Georgette in the sunless alleys between the shops and businesses, and squinting into the distance hoping to see the girl somewhere. Anywhere.

What had happened to her? Had she gone back to the saloon, or had even more misfortune found her?

CHAPTER 12

"Fool calf somehow got his head stuck in the fence," Jason called out to Elise as he came into the house and hung his hat on the hook behind the door. "It was a good thing Roy happened to be nearby and heard the ruckus."

He wandered into the kitchen where he assumed she was preparing supper. He stopped dead in the doorway when he saw her.

She was slumped at the table, her head lowered, the sheet of paper he assumed was the letter from her mother in her lap. "What's wrong?" he asked, crossing the room toward her. "Bad news?"

She shook her head and looked up at him. Tears spiked her lashes and her cheeks were flushed.

"No," she choked out. "Everyone is fine."

"Then what's wrong?"

She shook her head as a fresh wave of tears filled

her eyes and rolled down her cheeks. "I just … I just miss them."

Jason understood that. His parents had been killed when he was sixteen, and there were still days he missed them so much his chest hurt. He even missed his brother, the only family he had left. They'd been bitter enemies growing up, but their relationship had changed once they were adults. Then Travis had gone to Colorado to make his fortune mining for silver and over the years, their letters had grown fewer and further between. He hadn't heard from him in almost a year. "I know."

Even though Elise's mother and sisters were still very much alive, they were so far away they might as well be dead.

She let out a brittle laugh. "And I miss that horrible apartment that always smelled like cabbage from the Ukrainian family down the hall, and the noise from the children in the apartment next to ours. How is it possible to miss something I couldn't wait to leave?"

His insides twisted at the pain and sadness on Elise's beautiful face. He wanted to tell her he'd make sure she never had to feel sad again, but he couldn't promise that.

But he did make a promise to himself. If there was anything he could do to make sure he never had to see tears in her eyes again, he'd do it.

Right now, though, he couldn't conjure up her family and all he could do was try to comfort her.

Taking the letter out of her grasp, he put it on the table. Then he took her hands in his and brought her to her feet.

Slowly, he drew her toward him, wrapping his arms around her until she was resting against him. Her scent filled his nose, her soft curls brushing against his face.

She sagged against him, her tears dampening his shirt, her sniffles growing quieter.

Heat spread through him. Her soft curves molded against him and he wanted nothing more than to kiss her. He resisted. This wasn't the time, and if—no, when—the time came that he did kiss her, he'd be sure she wanted it as much as he did.

He held her gently and murmured, "I'm sorry, honey. I wish I could bring your family to you, but I can't. Maybe one day, but not right now."

He felt her nod against his chest. "I know," she said, her voice muffled.

She looked up at him, sniffled once more and blinked back her tears. "Thank you for … understanding."

"I do."

She looked up at him, blinking her tears away. "Maybe there's some way I can save some money myself …"

"We've already talked about this," he said. "I don't want you working. You have enough to do taking care of the house and Beth. Maybe in a couple of years I can come up with the money to send for them. Just not now."

She pulled out of his arms and straightened. Brushing the backs of her hands over her eyes, she nodded. "I'll go and start supper."

Then she spun around and walked away.

Beth sat on the floor, the rag ball clutched in her tiny fingers. Elise had sewn it the night before from a small piece of fabric she'd found in a dresser and then stuffed it with rags.

Beth loved it, and once Elise showed her how to roll it across the floor, the baby had spent the entire morning trying to roll it and then chasing after it. When she caught it, she held it up in triumph, looked up at Elise and grinned.

Elise watched, laughing. Beth's smile made her day brighter, and even though she still missed her own family, she'd overcome her bout of homesickness, and over the past few days she'd deliberately kept herself so busy she didn't have time to think about her family back East.

The ball rolled under a large cabinet near the fireplace. Beth tried to reach it but when she realized she couldn't, she wriggled herself into a sitting position on the floor. Her cheeks reddened and a frown creased her forehead. Her bottom lip quivered in a pout, and a few moments later, she began to sob, her cries growing louder with each passing second.

Elise put down her mending and lowered herself to her hands and knees to try to retrieve the ball.

Suddenly, the front door opened. Assuming it was Jason, she continued to contort herself into every position she could think of so that she could reach the ball.

Roy's voice overpowered Beth's cries. "Uh … you need some help?" he asked.

Mortified to be caught with her backside in the air, Elise scrambled to her feet. Her cheeks burned. "Oh … I was just …"

Beth's wails grew louder.

"Something you need under there?" Roy asked, crossing the room.

Elise nodded. "Beth's ball."

"Okay," Roy said, "let me try. My arms are longer than yours."

Elise looked on as Roy stretched out on the floor and reached under the cabinet. A few seconds later, he slid his arm out, the ball in his hand.

Beth's cries stopped immediately when Roy gave her the ball.

Elise frowned as the realization struck her that this might have been the baby's first tantrum. Elise wasn't sure how to deal with it and made a mental note to ask for Tillie's advice as soon as possible.

"I didn't expect you," Beth said. "What brings you by?"

"Jason asked me to stop in and see if you need anything in town. I need to buy washing powder so the boys can do their laundry tonight. I'd be happy to pick something up for you while I'm there if there's anything you want."

"No, but thank you for offering."

"No problem." He touched the brim of his hat with his finger and then turned and left, closing the door behind him.

Elise couldn't sleep, thoughts of ways to help Georgette spinning in her mind. Finally, after tossing and turning for more than two hours, she got up, crept down the stairs and into the kitchen.

She poured herself a cup of milk and took two sugar cookies she'd made that afternoon out of the tin on the shelf.

She slid into a chair at the table, a half-formed idea that had come to her during the night taking shape in her brain—an idea that would help Georgette to leave the saloon and while at the same time, give Elise an income that she could use to send for her mother and sisters. Could it really work?

For a few seconds, she pondered whether to tell Jason about what she was planning to do, but decided against it until she tried it out herself and she was sure she could handle it.

Right now, the ranch hands did their own laundry,

which cut into their time off. Would they be willing to pay her and Georgette to do their laundry for them? She knew far too well how to scrub clothes and iron. In fact, she'd been praised for her ironing skills. Not that the ranch hands would likely care if there was a crease in a shirt.

It wouldn't interfere with her regular chores and wouldn't even take up space in the house since Jason had built a wash house with a boiler to make it easy.

If Georgette had never done laundry, Elise could teach her.

If Roy and the other hands agreed, she and Georgette would take over, and if that worked out well, they could even start offering the service to the hands at the other ranches nearby.

She didn't like the thought of keeping her plan a secret from Jason, but he'd made it clear a few weeks before that he didn't approve of her getting a job.

But this isn't really a job, she reasoned. It's a business. Surely he wouldn't object to her running her own business. After all, Miranda was a married woman and she worked alongside her husband. Elise couldn't really do that since she wasn't physically strong enough to do ranch work, but she could have a business of her own—at least temporarily.

"What are you doing up?"

Jason's voice startled her. Her hand flew to her chest as she twisted in her chair to see him come into the kitchen.

"Oh ..." Heat washed over her as her gaze

landed on his bare chest. She'd never seen a man in such a state of undress before. Her father had always worn a nightshirt to sleep in. She'd assumed all men wore them so she was shocked to learn that Jason slept in only a pair of drawers and nothing else.

"Is everything all right?" he asked.

She nodded. "I …" Everything was all right until you came in, she almost blurted out but managed to stop herself. Now, looking at him with his hair all tousled and his jaw shadowed with hair, everything was definitely not all right.

She'd been attracted to a man once before, but never like this. Sensations that were unfamiliar filled her from her head to her toes. "Yes, everything's fine," she lied. "I had trouble sleeping, that's all."

"Something on your mind?"

She shook her head. "Just restless, but I think I can sleep now." She got up and moved toward the doorway. As she passed him, her hand brushed his arm. The muscle beneath his skin tensed beneath her fingers. Her nerve endings tingled.

She looked up, her eyes meeting his. His dark blue gaze seemed to see right into her soul, to be able to know exactly how she felt.

Suddenly, his hands gripped her shoulders. His mouth lowered to hers and his lips claimed hers.

She couldn't think. Couldn't breathe. She was lost.

She'd never been kissed before. Sure, she'd thought about what it might feel like, but even her wildest imagination didn't come close to the reality of his kiss.

His tongue ran along the seam of her lips. As if they moved without her even thinking about it, she parted her lips and his tongue slipped inside, tangling with hers.

Awareness surged through her. She loved the way his lips felt on hers, and his short whiskers grazed her skin, heightening her senses.

She wound her arms around his neck, her fingers toying with the honey-colored hair at his nape.

He drew her close, so close that she was pressed against his bare skin with only the thin cotton of her nightdress between them.

Her heart pounded. Or was it his?

She couldn't resist touching the skin on his shoulders and his back, delighting in the play of muscles as they shifted beneath her touch.

He dragged his lips from hers and planted soft kisses down the side of her neck. Her knees threatened to buckle beneath her.

"Jason …" She gasped, unable to draw a deep breath.

Suddenly, he released her, taking a step back and shaking his head. "Oh, I'm so sorry …"

"It's …" How could she tell him this had been the most exciting thing that had ever happened to her?

"I promised you the day we got married that I wouldn't expect anything from you. I never intended to kiss you like that and I shouldn't have. I'm sorry."

He seemed about to say something else, but then changed his mind, turned and left the room.

CHAPTER 13

Jason swung the axe in an arc, the blade splitting the log and sending splinters flying into the air. He'd been chopping wood for hours and his muscles burned from the exertion, but if he was tired enough, maybe he'd be able to sleep again.

Since the night he'd kissed Elise, he hadn't had a decent night's sleep. Her face filled his dreams, the memory of her lips against his sending him for more quick dips in the river than he could count.

He wanted her in his bed. He could easily admit that. But it was more than lust. He'd fallen in love with her, with her kindness, her devotion to Beth, the way she nibbled her lip when she was worried and even her off-key singing when she thought he was out of earshot. In fact, there wasn't much about her he didn't love.

And he was furious with himself for letting

himself love her. He'd been so sure he could never love another woman after what Irene had done to him, but somehow, Elise's sweetness had gotten behind the wall he'd built around his heart.

She could destroy him now. He'd promised himself that he'd never give another woman that kind of power, and without him even realizing it, he'd handed it to Elise on a silver platter.

He swore.

Something had happened to the friendship Elise had thought she and Jason were building. Everything had changed between them since the night he kissed her. While he was still kind and considerate, he stayed out of her way except at mealtimes.

They were strangers again. If she happened to brush past him or even come close to touching his hand or arm, he jerked away from her as if she were a leper.

There was only one reason she could think of why he'd changed—he hadn't liked their kiss.

She had no experience in kissing so she must have done it wrong. Still, he knew she'd never had a suitor so he couldn't expect her to know how to kiss properly.

Or maybe she hadn't reacted to it the way she was supposed to. Her body heated as she recalled the kiss, the way her lips had tingled, her heart had raced and strange sensations had filled every part of her.

She wanted to kiss him again, more than anything. And she wanted to know what happened after kissing. What else happened between a man and a woman? If a kiss could make her toes curl, what would the rest do to her?

Oh, how she wished Juliette was here so that she could ask about it. Did Juliette feel the same way when her fiancé kissed her? Or was what Elise feeling so unusual, and that was why Jason stayed away from her now?

Hopefully she'd have enough money before winter arrived in the north to send for her mother and her sisters, and she'd be able to find out everything she needed to know.

By the time Elise went into town three weeks later, she'd already done laundry for Jason's men and also for some of the ranch hands at Stonehaven, the spread Neall and Audra Gardiner owned nearby.

Twice, she'd had to creep out of the house late at night to finish, and it was only a matter of time before Jason caught her. She hated to keep what she was doing a secret, but she had no choice since he'd been so firm about her not working.

She hadn't earned enough money until now to

help Georgette escape the saloon, but now, it was time.

She planned to hurry through her shopping at the mercantile, find Georgette and explain her proposition and be back at the ranch long before supper.

Unfortunately, the mercantile was busy when she arrived, and by the time she'd put her purchases in the wagon bed, she was already later than she expected.

As she approached the saloon, Elise glanced at the balcony where several women were calling out to the men on the street.

Her gaze scanned the faces, her heart jolting when she saw Georgette, dressed in a purple satin dress that revealed much more than any decent woman showed. Georgette stood back from the edge of the balcony as if she was trying to hide herself from view.

A door opened and a fierce-looking giant of a man appeared on the balcony and stormed toward Georgette. She took a step back from him, but he grabbed her arm and dragged her inside.

Elise's heart squeezed. If she'd had any doubts about what she was doing, she didn't now. She'd deal with Jason if and when she had to.

Tugging on the reins, she stopped the wagon and climbed down. Her heart raced and her knees quivered, but she marched across the street, took in a few deep calming breaths and pushed through the batwing doors of the saloon.

Mon Dieu! How could anyone breathe in the cloud

of smoke and the odor of unwashed bodies hanging in the air?

A few men sat at one table, and a balding man stood behind the bar wiping glasses with a towel that looked as if it hadn't been laundered in months.

Standing beside him was the man she'd seen with Georgette on the balcony. His gaze raked over her, but she held her head high and strode toward him.

"Looking for a job?" he asked, practically leering at her.

"Absolutely not," she replied, annoyed that she couldn't prevent the nervous quiver in her voice. "I'm here to speak to Georgette."

"Is that so?" He and the bartender exchanged glances. "She's busy right now."

Elise could only imagine what was keeping her busy, and her stomach roiled. "How long will she be?"

He shrugged. "Depends. What do you want her for?"

"Then I'll wait," she replied, ignoring his question. A faint smile tugged at her lips as she moved away, pushed open the door and stopped on the boardwalk right in front of the saloon entrance. She had the feeling he wouldn't be happy to have a woman—a respectable woman—greeting his customers.

"You can't wait there," he called out to her. "My customers can't get in."

She took two steps to the side, out of the way. He couldn't complain now about her being in the way.

Silence fell on the saloon. As she waited, twice, a man approached and, seeing her standing there, walked away.

She was sure the owner had noticed it, too.

It didn't take long before Georgette stepped outside.

Turning to the owner, Elise smiled sweetly as she took Georgette's arm and led her away.

Dusk was falling by the time Elise got back to the ranch. Jason was on the porch, Beth in his arms, when she drew the horses to a stop and got out of the wagon.

"I'll have supper on the table in a few minutes," she said, hurrying past him into the house.

Jason followed behind. "Where have you been? I was worried."

The accusing tone of his voice told Elise he was more angry than concerned about her safety. "I was in town. It just took longer than I expected."

"You said you were going to the mercantile."

She forced a laugh, hoping it would lighten the tension that seemed to be building. "I did. It was busier than usual and Dorothea was a chatterbox. I'm sorry if you were worried."

Did he believe her? She wasn't lying…well, not really. She just wasn't telling him the whole truth of where she'd been.

Georgette had been so happy to see her, and once Elise had explained her plan, the girl had been more than eager to go with her. Leaving her belongings behind until she was settled, Elise took her to a boarding house at the other end of town.

Elise used some of her own money to pay for a room in advance, and had pressed a few coins in Georgette's hands and extracted a promise from Georgette to come to the ranch the next morning. It would be a fair walk from town, but Georgette was young and had assured Elise that she'd be there.

Elise didn't mention any of that to Jason. She would tell him everything soon, but not yet.

"It doesn't take three hours to go to the mercantile and back, even if the store was busy."

"Where else do you think I went?" she asked sweetly.

"I don't know …"

"Am I a prisoner here that I need to account for every moment of my time?"

"Of course not."

She met his gaze. "Then what exactly is the problem?"

Without waiting for an answer, she took Beth out of his arms and marched away, muttering to herself.

"What?" Jason asked from the doorway.

She turned to face him. "Excuse me?"

"You're speaking French again," he pointed out. "You know I don't understand what you're saying. What did you say?"

For that, she was glad. She wasn't about to tell him she'd been calling him a few names she wouldn't say out loud, not the least of which was that he was acting like a horse's behind.

She settled Beth in her high chair and took a skillet off the shelf. "Nothing important."

~

"There's something she's not telling me." While Jason held the fence post steady, Roy set the nail and hammered it into the wood.

"Really," Roy murmured past the nails he held between his lips while Jason crossed to the wagon to get another piece of lumber.

"I think she's seeing another man," Jason went on once he got back and was placing the slat into position.

Roy took the nails out of his mouth. "You're crazy. What makes you think that?"

"I don't know … the way she's acting …"

"I haven't noticed anything different," Roy said. "She seems the same whenever I see her."

Jason slid a glance at Roy. How often did he see Elise? Was that guilt in his eyes? Was it possible history was repeating itself? Elise and Roy …?

His stomach clenched and his breath caught. It couldn't be happening again. He'd never survive losing her, too.

"You're out of your mind," Roy repeated. "It's all in your imagination."

"It's not. She's not herself …"

"I hate to be the one to tell you, but you're not yourself lately either."

He supposed that was true. He hadn't been thinking straight since the night he'd kissed Elise. He shouldn't have done it. Even in that split second before his mouth covered hers, he knew it was a bad idea. That it would change everything.

But he'd done it anyway. And he'd been right. It had changed everything between them.

Ever since, he'd regretted kissing her, not because he hadn't liked it, but because he had. He'd liked it too much. Now, when he closed his eyes at night, her face filled his thoughts and dreams, making it hard to sleep soundly.

Which was why he'd woken up when he heard her open her bedroom door and tiptoe down the stairs and go outside.

Those sounds definitely weren't his imagination. She had to be with another man, and the thought of it made his stomach clench in anger and his chest tighten. If not that, what other reason could she have for sneaking out at night once he was asleep?

He wouldn't accuse her of anything until he was sure, though. Next time she left the house when she thought he was asleep, he'd be waiting when she got back.

"That's everything for this week, gentlemen," Elise said as set the last pile of clean clothes on one of the cots in the bunkhouse. "All laundered and ironed."

Roy came to stand beside her. "Thanks, Elise. It's sure nice to not have to do our own." Roy and two of the other hands began sorting through the pile and taking out those that belonged to them.

"Here you go," Roy said, handing her an envelope containing her payment. "I still don't feel right about keeping this from Jason, but I will."

Elise smiled. "You have no idea how much I appreciate it. In another few weeks, I'll have enough for train fare for my family. After that, Georgette will take care of your laundry herself and it won't matter if Jason knows about it."

Leaving the bunkhouse a few minutes later, she looked up at the ebony sky. With only a sliver of moonlight to light her way, she moved carefully on the uneven ground, praying she didn't meet up with any animals that roamed around in the night.

A movement on the porch caught her attention. Fear skittered up her spine. What kind of animal was wandering around up there?

"Have a nice time?"

Her heart did a somersault in her chest when she heard Jason's voice coming from the shadows. While she was relieved to know there were no wild animals ready to attack her, the harshness in his voice unnerved her.

Her stomach clenched, and her blood rushed to her ears. "What are you doing out here?"

"Answer my question."

She stopped at the bottom of the porch stairs, the first bubbles of her own anger building in her stomach. She'd answer his question. "You asked if I had a nice time," she began, her voice sharp and her words clipped. "No, I did not have a nice time. Finishing the wash I didn't get to today because Beth was fussy isn't my idea of having a good time."

It wasn't really a lie, she justified to herself. She had been finishing the ironing she'd planned to do that afternoon after Georgette left to go back to town. And Beth was teething again, so she'd been clingy and whiny all day.

"You were finishing the laundry," he repeated. His tone made it very clear he didn't believe her.

"I was."

"Then why did I see you coming out of the bunkhouse a minute ago?"

Zut! He'd caught her! What was she going to say?

If she told him the truth, all her work so far would have been for nothing. She hated to lie, but she still had time to earn enough money so her family could get to Texas before winter. All she needed was a couple more weeks …

Elise's heart jolted. "I … I took some cake …"

"At this time of night?"

"It was the first chance I had."

"I've told you before to stay away from the men."

Elise bristled. No one, not even her husband, would dictate who she could speak to. "Why not, Jason? What do you think I'm doing?"

"Just stop going over there."

She climbed the porch stairs until she was face to face with him. In the glow from the lamplight coming through the window, his face was in shadow, but she didn't need to see it. She knew exactly how he looked right now—his jaw tense, his eyes narrowed. "Why?" she prodded. "Why does it upset you so much that I speak to your ranch hands and take some dessert over there once in a while?"

"I don't have to give you a reason," he spat out. "I'm your husband and I'm telling you to stay away from them."

She took a step back, her temper rising. "Or else what, Jason? What are you going to do? Punish me like I'm a child who needs disciplined?"

He didn't speak, didn't move for what seemed like minutes, but was only a few seconds. His voice was much softer when he finally answered. "Just don't."

He spun around and stormed off, leaving her standing on the porch, his words echoing in her brain.

Jason had a feeling Elise was going to call his bluff. Even in the shadowy light coming through the window, he'd seen the fury in her eyes and heard the challenge in her voice.

He'd never tried to control Irene's actions, and he'd suffered because of it. He couldn't let the same thing happen again, but when he really thought about it, by dictating where Elise went and who she spoke to, that was exactly what he was trying to do. He'd turned into a bully.

She had a mind of her own. He should have realized that any woman who would leave their home and family and travel alone to a strange place to marry a man she didn't know must have courage and strength. Even if his suspicions were nothing more than his imagination, if he tried to domineer her, he was going to lose her.

But could he accept her explanations and try to put their friendship—and their marriage—first?

Elise was struggling to put a bonnet on Beth's head with one hand while at the same time holding the baby still so she didn't topple off the bed. "You really have to stop squirming," she said with a laugh.

Beth responded by digging her heels into the mattress and scooting away, giggling.

"Something funny?" Jason asked, appearing in the doorway, looking so handsome it almost took her breath away.

"Beth doesn't want a bonnet on and she's letting me know," Elise replied.

"She doesn't like to sit still at all, does she?" he commented, crossing the room to hold Beth still while Elise tied the bow on the bonnet.

When they were finished, Jason took out his pocket watch and glanced at it. "Are you almost ready to go? We're going to be late if we don't leave soon."

Elise yawned. She'd been in the wash house until late doing laundry and had gotten up before dawn to make breakfast and get herself and Beth dressed for church.

While Georgette did most of the work, Elise joined her when Jason was away from the house. Between the two of them, the laundry business was going better than she'd dreamed, and she almost had enough money to pay the train fare for her family. She only hoped Jason didn't find out about the business before she was ready.

Georgette kept most of the profits, which was only fair since she was doing most of the work. She was still living at Mrs. Humphrey's boarding house and was slowly learning to speak English. One of the soiled doves at the saloon had collected Georgette's few belongings for her, and Georgette had mentioned to Elise that one day when she was established, she'd like to help the other ladies.

She nodded. "Coming," she replied.

Jason crossed the room and studied her face. "Are you sick?" he asked. "You don't look well."

She wasn't sick. She was exhausted, but she couldn't admit that.

"I'm fine." Pasting a smile on her face, she met his gaze.

Concern filled his eyes and a slight frown creased his forehead. "Are you sure? I don't want you getting sick."

"I know. You need me to look after Beth and the house." Elise recognized that her voice was sharp, but she couldn't help herself. She wanted to be more than a housekeeper and a nanny and she didn't know how to make Jason love her the way she loved him.

"It's not that …" he began. "I … never mind. Let's go. We don't want to walk in after the service has started."

As they settled into the wagon a few minutes later and started down the trail toward town, Jason said, "I want to hear the sermon today. He's talking about the ten commandments."

"He's been doing that for a few weeks now," Elise pointed out.

"I know, but today he's talking about adultery. Should make some people sit up and pay attention."

Several more weeks passed. Jason had noticed there was a pattern to Elise's after-dark disappearances. Each week, she left the house on Wednesday and Saturday nights.

He wanted to confront her, and even though he'd tried to tamp down the jealous knot in his stomach, he'd failed. His jealousy was eating away at him until they were barely speaking to each other.

But he kept quiet, a plan forming in his mind. He'd follow her on Saturday night when he knew the men would be spending the evening in town like they always did.

One Saturday afternoon, he took Bobby, the youngest of the ranch hands, aside when the other men were out moving cattle. The boy was barely sixteen and hadn't been working at the ranch long enough to get involved with Elise.

"What is it, boss?" Bobby asked, his voice quivering. "You gonna fire me?"

Jason shook his head. "I want you to come to the house at nine o'clock tonight, but stay outside in the shadows until I come and get you."

"Sure, but what's going on?"

"Elise is going out tonight and I have to leave the house for a few minutes. I want you to keep an eye on

Beth while I'm gone. She'll be sleeping, but just in case she wakes up, somebody needs to be there."

The boy nodded. "Okay." He turned away.

"And Bobby," Jason called out after him. "This is between you and me. Nobody else needs to know what you're doing."

CHAPTER 15

$\mathcal{J}$ason heard Elise's bedroom door open late that night. He waited, listening to her footsteps on the stairs and the door open and quietly close.

Throwing the thin blanket off, he got out of bed and moved to the window. The moon was full, making it easy to follow her shadowy figure as she disappeared behind the barn.

His chest burned, feeling so tight it was hard to draw a breath.

For several minutes, he sat on the edge of the bed. He had to know.

As he left the house, Bobby appeared out of the shadows. He nodded to the boy as he passed and watched until the boy went inside the house.

His anger built with every step as he stormed across the yard to the bunkhouse. This time … this time he'd kill the ranch hand his wife was seeing behind his back. And then he'd throw her out, let her work at the saloon since she was nothing better than a soiled dove anyway.

He threw open the bunkhouse door and stormed inside.

He couldn't breathe. Couldn't move. Couldn't think past what he was seeing—Roy and Elise. Alone. Together. Roy's shirt lay in a heap on the bunk beside him, and he was putting money into Elise's outstretched hand.

He'd been right. Just as he'd suspected that day when he and Roy had talked about the change in Elise. How could Roy do this to him? He was his foreman, but more than that, Roy was his friend. How could this happen again?

The sound of the door slamming against the wall drew their attention and they both looked straight at him, guilt shining in their eyes.

"Ohh…" The sound came from Elise's lips.

"This isn't what it looks like …" Roy began.

Jason couldn't hear Roy's words past the blood pounding in his ears. His skin burned with rage.

"Listen, Jason …"

There were no excuses. Jason's hands clenched into fists. Without a word, he lunged toward Roy. His fist smashed into Roy's jaw.

Roy dropped to the floor, raising his hands to protect his face. Jason straddled him and hit him again. Blood spurted from Roy's lip and a bone cracked.

He lifted his arm to attack again.

"Jason!" Elise screeched in his ear as she tugged at his arm, trying to pull him away from Roy. "Stop!"

Something in her voice burst through the fury inside him. He paused, his arm in mid-air as he gazed down at Roy's battered face.

Slowly, he lowered his arm and got to his feet. "Get out," he hissed. "Now, before I kill you."

Roy opened his mouth to say something, but closed it again. He ran his hand over his jaw as he got to his feet, grabbed his shirt and hat, and left the bunkhouse.

As the door closed, he turned back to Elise.

"Jason …" Elise's voice was a plea. "Nothing was going on."

His brows lifted. "He was standing with you, half naked, and you were taking money from him and you're trying to tell me nothing was going on."

"That's right."

"Sorry," he said in a tone that told her the word was definitely not an apology, "but I don't buy that for a minute."

She sighed and took a step toward him. "This is all my fault, and Roy deserves an apology. I should have told you sooner. I know that now."

Jason's heart hitched. His throat tightened, almost choking him. "Told me what?"

"I should have told you that I've been doing his laundry. His and the other men, as well as some of the men from Stonehaven. What you saw was him paying me for doing his laundry. That's all."

"You really expect me to believe that."

"I do." She frowned. "I'm so sorry I kept it from you, but I do expect you to believe me when I tell you something, not to make up stories in your head."

"I'm not making anything up," he protested. "I saw you with him, and he was half naked. His shirt—"

"I offered to mend a tear in it for him. That's all."

Was she telling the truth? Had he almost killed one of his best friends because of his imagination?

Elise's voice softened. "Why don't you trust me? Why do you think I'd betray you?"

He gazed at her, her expression so innocent. But Irene had pulled the wool over his eyes for months. He'd never suspected at thing. "I have my reasons."

"I need to know what those reasons are. I need to understand—"

"No, you don't. You need to accept that I don't trust anyone."

She stared at him for what seemed a long time, her eyes filling with tears. Finally, she tucked the money into the pocket of her skirt. "That's not good enough, Jason. I've given you no reason to think I'd betray you, and I can't live with someone who doesn't trust me. I'll pack my things and leave in the morning."

Elise stood at the bedroom window in the Fords' house watching the storm raging outside, the same room she'd stayed in when she'd first arrived in Sapphire Springs.

Then, she'd been filled with hope and had been looking forward to her future with Jason and Beth. Now, all that was left was regret and guilt and a future filled with pain and loss.

She'd been staying with Micah and Tillie for three days, and she could barely even think about the events of that night without guilt almost suffocating her. Not only had she destroyed her marriage, she'd been responsible for Roy losing his job and his home as well almost getting him killed. She was lucky Jason hadn't killed him. Somehow, she'd have to learn to live with that guilt.

The day before, she'd gone to see Georgette. The girl had been surprised to find Elise in the parlor of the boarding house, and had burst into tears when she'd learned what happened, which made Elise feel even worse.

She'd ruined everything for everyone. Beth would forget her. She knew that. But she'd never forget Beth and her heart ached to hold the precious child one more time.

Elise's misery was physically painful, and for the first time, she wondered if it was perhaps true that people could die from a broken heart. Because hers wasn't only broken, it was shattered. And there was nothing she could do about it.

Yes, she could beg Jason's forgiveness, and he might take her back, but at what cost? She loved him more than she'd ever thought it was possible to love another human being, but she couldn't bear to see suspicion in his eyes whenever he looked at her, to be questioned about her movements, to know that no matter how long they were married or how devoted she was to him, he would always believe she would betray him.

And what about Beth? How could she help Jason raise Beth in a home filled with mistrust and suspicion? She couldn't do that to the child she'd come to love, no matter how much it hurt to leave.

A light knock sounded at the door.

"Come in," she said quietly.

The door opened. Elise moved away from the window as Tillie came into the room and set a tray on the small table in the corner. "You need to eat something," she said.

Elise gave a cursory glance at the light meal Tillie had brought. "Thank you, but I'm really not hungry."

"Did you get any sleep at all last night?" Tillie asked, crossing to the window.

Elise shook her head. How could she sleep when her life was in tatters around her?

Tillie took her hand and gave it a sympathetic squeeze. "I won't pry," she said, "but if you need someone to talk to, I'm here."

Elise still hadn't told Tillie the reason she'd left Jason, only that it didn't work out and she'd be going back to New York. She had the money for the fare, so all she had to do was wait for the next stage to take her to Austin where she could catch the train.

As Tillie turned to leave, Elise called out to her. "Tillie, I would like to tell you what happened."

Tillie gave her a gentle smile. "Then let's have a scone and some tea while we're talking."

Elise nodded, tears filling her eyes as she began to speak. "He doesn't trust me," Elise said through shuddery breaths when she was finished, "and he won't tell me why."

"I won't offer you any advice unless you want it," Tillie said softly.

Elise blinked back the tears filling her eyes. "I do."

"Don't leave without talking to him one more time," she said. "Perhaps he's had a change of heart and is too proud to beg. If, after talking to him again, you feel the same way, then go back to your family."

Elise nodded. Tillie was right. She had to see him again. That night, they'd both been angry, hurt. Now, in the clear light of day, she knew she couldn't walk away from Jason and Beth and their life together unless she was sure there was no way to salvage their marriage.

Jason sank into the chair and took a bite of the sandwich he'd made for lunch, forcing himself to eat even though eating was the last thing he felt like doing these days.

After what seemed like hours of sobbing, Beth had finally cried herself to sleep and the house was quiet.

He'd never noticed the profound silence in the house as much as he did now that Elise was gone. Sure, it had been quiet before he'd married Elise, but it had never felt so … empty. Now it felt as if the heart of the house was missing.

Four days. It had been four days since she left, and it hurt, so much more than he'd expected. The morning she left, he'd wanted to ask her to stay, to forgive him, but he hadn't. He'd let her go, even though he'd been so heartsick, his whole chest had ached.

He didn't want to want her. He didn't want to need her more than air. He didn't want to dream about her every time he fell into an exhausted sleep. But he did, and every day was getting worse, to the point he didn't even want to close his eyes at night.

Tonight would be no different. He knew that.

Draining his coffee, he got up and was putting his dishes in the dry sink when a knock sounded at the door.

When he opened it, he was surprised to see Tucker Gates, the foreman at Stonehaven Ranch, on the porch. "Afternoon, Tucker," he said. "Come on in."

"Jason," Tucker said, stepping into the house. "I…"

Jason noticed that Tucker's eyes were scanning the room as if he was searching for something, or someone. "Uh … I went to the bunkhouse but nobody's there…"

"No, the men are taking the cattle up to the north pasture today. Something I can do for you?"

"No…well, maybe…"

Jason's irritation was building. What was wrong with him? He'd never known Tucker to be at a loss for words. "Spit it out, whatever it is."

"The laundry…I brought the laundry."

Laundry!

Jason's throat tightened. The lunch he'd eaten sat like a lead ball in his stomach. "The laundry?"

Tucker nodded. "I…I'm not supposed to say anything, but—"

"Elise is doing your laundry." Jason turned away from the door, raking his hands through his hair, his heartbeat racing.

She'd been telling the truth, and instead of believing her—trusting her—he'd accused her of being unfaithful and he'd seriously injured Roy.

How could he have been such a fool? He'd driven away the woman he loved and lost a friend because of his jealousy.

"You all right?" Tucker's voice filtered into his thoughts.

He turned to face Tucker and nodded. "Yeah. Fine. Elise isn't here so she can't do it right now."

"Okay," Tucker replied. "I'll let the boys know. Maybe next week…"

Jason didn't reply. He should tell Tucker there would be no more laundry service, that Elise was gone, but he couldn't bring himself to do that. "Sure."

With a nod, Tucker turned and descended the stairs. Jason stood in the doorway and watched as the wagon rolled away, his mind whirling.

He should have believed Elise when she'd told him nothing was going on between her and Roy. He should have trusted her.

Irene's betrayal had filled him with bitterness, grief and pain. He'd suffered so much because of her that it terrified him to truly give himself to another woman, to be vulnerable. All he'd done was allow her to destroy his life again, even from beyond the grave.

It was time to take away Irene's power over him and to let himself love again, trust again. To fully give himself to Elise.

Somehow, he knew he had to find a way to convince Elise to forgive him, to give him another chance. If it wasn't too late.

CHAPTER 16

*E*lise added flour to the bowl and carefully blended it into the liquid for the cake she'd offered to make for dessert. "It's time," she said to Tillie, who was filling the coffee pot with water. "It's time. I'm going to go and see Jason tomorrow."

Tillie finished pouring the water and then turned to face Elise. "I'm glad, and hopefully the two of you can find a way to work through whatever the problem is."

"I doubt that's going to happen, but then I can go back to New York knowing I tried."

"Are you sure you want to go back East?"

Elise laughed inwardly. She wasn't sure of anything right now, but it seemed like the most logical thing to do was to go home. There was nothing left for her here in Sapphire Springs, and she couldn't bear to stay, loving him from afar, seeing him on the street or in church and knowing he hated her.

In a way, she could understand why. Her actions had been suspicious, and she had kept secrets from him. Still, he should have believed her when she'd told him the truth.

And he hadn't. He hadn't trusted her enough to put his suspicions aside.

It was for the best, she'd tried to tell herself as she lay awake at night, her tears soaking her pillow.

She dipped the cup back into the sack of flour and filled it, ready to add to the cake batter.

Suddenly, a knock sounded at the door. Startled, she jumped, her hand jerk and the flour spilled, dusting the table.

Tillie crossed to the door and opened it. Jason stood in the entrance, Beth in his arms.

Elise's heart slammed into her throat. He looked tired, haggard. She didn't see anger in his eyes like she had the night before she left, but the emotion in them was one she didn't recognize.

No one spoke for a long, silent beat. "Come in, Jason," Tillie said quietly.

Jason came inside, his gaze settling on Elise. "Hi, Elise."

As soon as the baby saw Elise, she grinned, let out a squeal and held out her arms.

How she'd missed that child! Hurrying to the door, Elise gathered Beth up into her arms and snuggled her against her chest, her heart swelling with love. How was she ever going to leave, knowing she'd never see Beth again?

Tillie turned toward Elise. "Why don't I take Beth into the other room so you two can talk?"

"Thanks," Jason said as Tillie reached for Beth.

What did he want? Just seeing him was almost unbearably painful.

"Will you come outside with me?" he asked after Tillie had left the room with Beth.

"Why?" Elise brushed the flour off her hands.

"Please?"

She was tempted to refuse, but when he opened the door, she crossed the room and brushed past him.

It was a perfect day, and any other time, she would have stopped to breathe in the perfume from the flowers in Tillie's garden, lift her face to soak up the sun's rays and enjoy the soft breeze on her skin. Not today, though. Today would be the last time she'd see Jason and Beth, and her entire body felt as if it were being torn apart.

She perched on the edge of one of the rocking chairs on the porch, her hands clasped in her lap. "What do you want, Jason?"

He crossed the porch and stood facing her, leaning against the railings. "I have something to say."

"You said everything there was to say the other night."

He shook his head. "I have three more words to say," he replied.

"What words?"

For a few seconds, he didn't say anything, his eyes boring into hers. Finally, his voice gruff as if he was speaking past a lump in his throat, he said, "I was wrong."

"What?"

"I was wrong," he repeated. "I know now that you were telling the truth, and I'm sorry, so very sorry, that I didn't believe you."

She looked away, trying to quell the emotions … so many emotions … surging through her. This was what she'd hoped for, prayed for. So why wasn't she thrilled to hear the words?

She suddenly realized she wanted more than he was capable of giving. "Thank you, Jason," she said softly.

He crossed to stand in front of her and took her hands in his. "Please come home. We miss you."

How she'd longed to hear those words, but she couldn't go back. She pulled her hands away. "No."

Jason's brow furrowed. Had he heard her right? She wouldn't come back to him, even though he'd admitted he was wrong?

"I can't," she repeated.

"Why not?"

His gaze met hers. A tear slid down her cheek. He made a move to brush it away but she jerked out of his reach and roughly ran the back of her hand across her face. "Because I can't live without trust."

"I told you I believe you."

"This time," she said. "What about next time?"

He didn't answer. What could he say? He couldn't promise something he wasn't sure he could deliver. All he could do was promise to try, but he didn't need to say the words to know that wouldn't be good enough.

He turned away and moved to the end of the porch, looking out over the garden and the fields beyond. He heard the chair squeak behind him and moments later, breathed in her lavender scent as she stood beside him. "I don't know why you don't trust me and you won't tell me why so I can understand," she went on. "And if I can't understand, then I can't come back."

He'd never told her about his marriage and about how Irene had deserted him and Beth. That had been a mistake. Maybe if Elise had known why it was so easy for him to jump to conclusions and assume the worst, she would have understood and none of this would have happened.

"What happened to you?"

He spun around to face her. "I was a fool," he ground out, his voice filled with bitterness. "The day I met Irene, I was instantly smitten, so blinded by her beauty and her charm that I fell instantly in love with her—or what I thought was love. I know now it wasn't real love. We kept company for a few weeks, and then I proposed to her. She said yes and we were married shortly after.

"The first few months of our marriage were happy, and when she came home from the doctor and told me she was expecting, I was sure we were going to have a perfect life."

"Then what happened?" Elise asked, taking a step closer.

"She wasn't happy about the pregnancy," he went on. "She got moody and distant and even moved out of our bedroom as she got closer to having the baby. She said it was because it was uncomfortable having someone sleep beside her. I missed her, but I thought that once the baby came, she'd be the woman I married again."

A bee buzzed nearby, and Elise waved it away. "I'm guessing that didn't happen."

Jason shook his head. "No. She went to visit her mother in Statesville regularly, or so she said. She left Beth with me while she was gone. I didn't suspect a thing until finally, after she'd gone for yet another 'visit', I found a note on the bureau. She'd left me and Beth and was going away with Grady Sprague, my best friend as well as being the foreman at one of the ranches on the other side of the river."

Elise's eyes widened. "I'm so … sorry …"

He let out a bitter laugh. "As if that wasn't bad enough, in the note she told me that Beth isn't even my child. She's Grady's."

"What?" Elise asked on a gasp.

He met Elise's gaze, seeing the same stunned expression he knew he must have had on his face when he'd first read Irene's note.

"She left Beth behind? Why?"

"Said she didn't like being a mother so it was best to leave Beth with me because she knew I'd look after her."

"How did she die?" Beth asked, although she wasn't really sure she wanted to know.

"A fire. She was with Grady and the sheriff said the curtains caught fire when they'd left an oil lamp too close."

"I can't imagine what you went through, and I only wish I'd known before … everything."

"Can you understand now why I wanted you to stay away from the bunkhouse?"

She nodded. "I do understand, but you're wrong to assume the same thing will happen again. I would never be unfaithful to you, and if you can't trust me completely, there's no future for us."

Elise's heart ached for Jason. He'd suffered so much more than most people, and now she'd hurt him, too.

Jason closed the gap between them. "Please come home. I need you. Beth needs you."

If only it were that simple … "I can't, Jason. I can't live with you without trust between us."

He dug his hands into his pockets and leaned against the porch railing. "You know, you didn't make it easy to trust you."

"What do you mean? I never—"

"You were so friendly with the boys. How could I

be sure what you had in mind, especially when you started going out at night? I didn't know you well, and you must admit, your actions were suspicious," he said. "You went against my wishes, you kept secrets from me, and you lied, maybe not with words but by not telling me the truth about what you were doing."

"I knew you wouldn't approve. You'd already told me not to get a job."

"So why did you?"

Tears threatened to fall, but she blinked them back. "I missed my mother and my sisters. I knew they'd be so much happier here … I wanted to earn enough money to send for them …"

"You could have asked me," he said. "I would have found a way if I'd known how important it was to you."

She shook her head. "You already worked so hard, I couldn't ask for more."

"So you disobeyed me."

A faint smile tweaked her lips. "I suppose I did."

"So you even lied when you made your vows at our wedding. What happened to love, honor … and obey?" He stressed the last word.

"Those vows aren't worth the breath it took to say them. We both lied."

"I didn't—"

"We vowed to love each other," she said softly.

He reached for her and cradled her face in his hands. "I do."

"What?"

"I didn't lie … well, I did at the time, but now I do love you …"

"You love me?" Elise's throat tightened and she blinked back tears that threatened to fall. *Zut!* She was crying again. She'd shed more tears in the past few days than in all the years since her father's death. She'd prayed for Jason's love, and that prayer had been answered. But there was no trust …

"Yes," he answered. "I do." He swore. "Lord knows I don't want to, but I do."

But you don't trust me?

"Can I believe you if you tell me there will be no more secrets?" he asked.

She frowned. "Of course. And you can believe me when I tell you I will never intentionally hurt you and that I will never be unfaithful to you. Because, you see, I love you, too. More than you'll ever know."

"Then I will trust you because I love you." He wrapped his arms around her waist, and she let herself fall into his embrace. She heard their heartbeats, beating in tandem, and her heart filled with joy.

He found her mouth, claiming it in a long kiss filled with the promise of a lifetime of love. When he finally released her, he drew back. "There is one thing," he said, a smile on his lips and his eyes filled with passion.

"What is it?" He'd given her the one thing she'd craved for so long—his love.

"Will you marry me?"

Elise giggled. "Don't be silly," she replied "We're already married."

"On paper, but will you *really* marry me?"

"What do you …?" she began, then realized what he was asking. Her face flamed, but excitement and anticipation for the future filled her heart.

"Oh, yes!" She stood on her tiptoes, cradled his face in her hands and kissed him. "I definitely will."

hristmas Day

Elise smiled contentedly as she watched Jason carving the turkey at the other end of the table. Her mother and Georgette sat on one side of the table, while Beth sat in her high chair between Juliette and Yvonne on the other.

Her family was complete … well, as complete as it could be for the time being. If her calculations were correct, next Christmas there would be another member of the family at the table, and she couldn't wait to tell Jason the news.

Her mother and sisters had arrived a few weeks before, and were already making friends in town. Georgette was running the laundry business herself, with a little help from Elise's mother when she needed it, and Yvonne was working with the only doctor in Sapphire Springs, trying to ease his workload.

Jason had apologized to Roy and had persuaded him to come back to the ranch, and just the week before, Elise had seen Juliette and Roy out walking near the river.

When the meal was over, Elise got up from the table and began to pick up the plates to take to the kitchen.

Jason stopped her, taking them from her hand and putting them back on the table. "Come with me."

"The dishes—"

"We shall take care of dishes," her mother said with a smile. "You go with Jason."

"But—"

Before she could object any further, Jason placed his hand on the center of her back and ushered her out of the house and across the yard to the barn.

The now-familiar smells greeted her as she stepped inside and let Jason lead her to a stall near the back of the barn. "Look!"

She leaned against the stall gate. There, inside the stall was a creamy-gold colored horse with a huge red ribbon around its neck.

"Ohhh …" Elise whispered. "She's beautiful, but why—?"

Jason wrapped an arm around her shoulder. "She's yours."

She turned to Jason, her eyes wide. "What?"

"I'm sorry your father wasn't able to give you a

pony of your own, so I wanted to give you one instead. There was only one problem. You're too big for a pony now. You need a horse you can ride. I didn't have any palominos, so I bought this one for you. Her name is Sunshine."

She couldn't believe what he was saying. "You bought her for me? My very own horse?"

He nodded. "Merry Christmas, sweetheart."

She looked up at Jason, seeing the love shining in his eyes, and her heart overflowed with so much love she could barely contain it.

"Thank you," she said past the lump forming in her throat. "This has been the most perfect Christmas ever."

"I'm glad. I want to give you everything you've ever dreamed of."

She reached up and wrapped her arms around his neck. "You already have," she said a moment before his lips lowered to hers in a kiss that promised her a future of unconditional love, trust and happiness.

Laura, the fifth book in the Mail-Order Brides of Sapphire Springs, is available now.

Can Laura continue to be married to a man who has no interest in love?

ABOUT THE AUTHOR

Margery Scott is the author of more than thirty books ranging from sweet historical western romance to spine-chilling thrillers. But no matter what genre she writes, every book has characters you can root for and a satisfying ending.

A transplanted Scot, Margery lives in Canada with her husband, but since she's a beach-lover at heart, she spends as much time as possible in the sunny south. When she's not writing, you can usually find her wielding a pool cue or a pair of knitting needles.

Website: www.margeryscott.com
Email: margery@margeryscott.com
Newsletter: www.margeryscott.com/newsletter
VIP Facebook reader group: www.facebook.com/groups/margeryscott

www.ingramcontent.com/pod-product-compliance
Lightning Source LLC
Chambersburg PA
CBHW030755200726
48288CB00004B/1182